ESCAPE FROM OBLIVION

by

Kim Kacoroski

ESCAPE FROM OBLIVION

Cover art illustrations by Kim Kacoroski, Natasha Kacoroski, Phillipe Velasquez, and Masha Tatarintsev

Visit the author website:
http://kimkacoroski.com

ISBN: 978-1-947036-10-9 (Paperback)

Version 2017.22.04

Book One of the Oblivion Series

Escape from Oblivion I

Other Books in the Oblivion Series

Beyond Oblivion II

Oblivion's Edge III

Oblivion's Deal IV

Flight from Oblivion V

Books in Flight Series

Flight from Oblivion I

Eagle's Flight in the American Revolution II

Flight of the Ascendants in the American Revolution III

Choices from the American Revolution IV

Bridges of Flight before the American Revolution V

Testimony VI

Books in the Camelon Series

The Promise of Camelon I

The Dragons of Camelon II

History of the World According to the Druids III

New Beginnings IV

Kingdom of the Golden Tara V

Bridges of Flight before the American Revolution VI

Introduction

This book has been written in urgency to create a safe home. As adults, people find it increasingly important to create a home, which will shelter and comfort them from the elements in society undermining their emotional and physical well-being. Consequently, this book represents a safe place, an environment which constructively addresses complex issues.

The best homes are based on visions. The vision may be nothing more than just a gleam in the future owner's eye, but homes are bought and chosen with respect to an imaginary dream house. Just like a home, this book is based on a vision. The idea for this vision came as the result of a movie called On a Clear Day. The movie depicted the story about a psychology professor who fell in love with a past reincarnation of one of his hypnotized students. Although the idea of reincarnation provided the inspiration, the notion of belonging proved more valuable: the idea that a person could attain such an understanding of themselves that all the pieces of events from the past, present, and future would fit together like a puzzle and present a vision of life so awesome and comprehensive that one would never question their place in the universe. Everything would be seen and understood for its own sake and life would just simply be enjoyed.

Initially this vision existed solely in the imagination. To achieve this vision, the limits prescribed by time and space needed to be transcended. In the imagination the past, present, and future can be fused together in one single moment. Once a place exists in the imagination for the vision, then the individual thinks of ways to make their imagination a reality by changing themselves or environment.

This ability to affect and change can be termed as the god-monkey duality: the god creates and the monkey imitates. For example, give a child some paper and crayons, and watch the child draw his/her universe. Give them some blocks and see them build their world, then destroy it. Yet, if mother leaves out her make-up or father forgets to put away his shoes, guess what the tot will be wearing next? Adults, on the other hand, generally imitate those who they also respect and create heroes specifically for this purpose. Even this type of imitation is limited and often a little more creativity is needed in order to succeed; when heroes fail, consult the muses.

So after musing over the challenge of transforming visions into reality, an individual resorts to the traditional means of achieving this, otherwise known as the human quest. Defining the human quest as a search for meaning in life through the interplay of creation and imitation, it can be pictured as a succession of people standing on the shoulders of the individual who came before them in time or effort. With each person the overall view of the world increases in scope, because each person can see a little bit further beyond the horizon than the next. As result, the base from which one chooses to stand on influences the viewpoint extracted. The only problem with the perspective gained by standing on another's shoulder is that there comes a point in the hierarchy where the individual begins to lose site of the original position.

However, clear day visions differ from human quests in that they prove more comprehensive. These visions require more than just the combined interplay of creation and imitation, they also recognize the individual's bond to the environment. Moreover, they are like instant camera shots where the flash of insight is so brief that if one ceased awareness, they would miss the significance of the impression on the senses. These impressions enable individuals to remember who they are and what they want out of life during the dark storms of confusion and self doubt.

Scientists have developed several physical explanations of clear day visions. Some physiologists refer to them as adrenalin produced highs. Other professionals claim that the vision occurs when the neurological impulse on one side of the brain becomes so forceful that it passes through the analytical side of the brain (without even a blink of an eye) and registers within the emotions connected to the abstract portion of the brain. Yet, a third group of scientists claim that clear day visions are a simply another mode of knowing. This description seems to most accurately account for the type of information perceived with clear day visions.

A psychologist from the third group, Robert Ornstein, asserts that there are different modes of knowing as concluded from his electroencephalogram studies of the brain. The different modes of knowing correspond to the functions of the left and right brain. In his book,

The Psychology of Consciousness, Ornstein claims that western societies use only one-half of their mental capacities because of the emphasis on language and logical thinking. Eastern societies tend to develop the left hemisphere of the brain through their intuitive and mystical cultures. He stresses that there are alternate ways of knowing which are ignored in the West. For this reason, tune references and author commentaries head the chapters.

Clear day visions result when the two modes of knowing unite in one mutual understanding, and it is one of those phenomena in life which one must accept in the imagination before making it possible in reality. All the trivial day to day details such as making breakfast, fighting the traffic, and getting to work on time, assume a new significance when placed in this birds-eye perspective. Major worldwide events such as war, hunger, and famine lose their despairing effect. Personal issues can be understood and accepted in a new light. Everyone has the capacity for clear day visions; the choice to use this perspective depends on the individual. What matters in life is an individual's response to reality because it generally reflects what one chooses to value. The story on the following pages reflects certain values, including a belief in clear day visions.

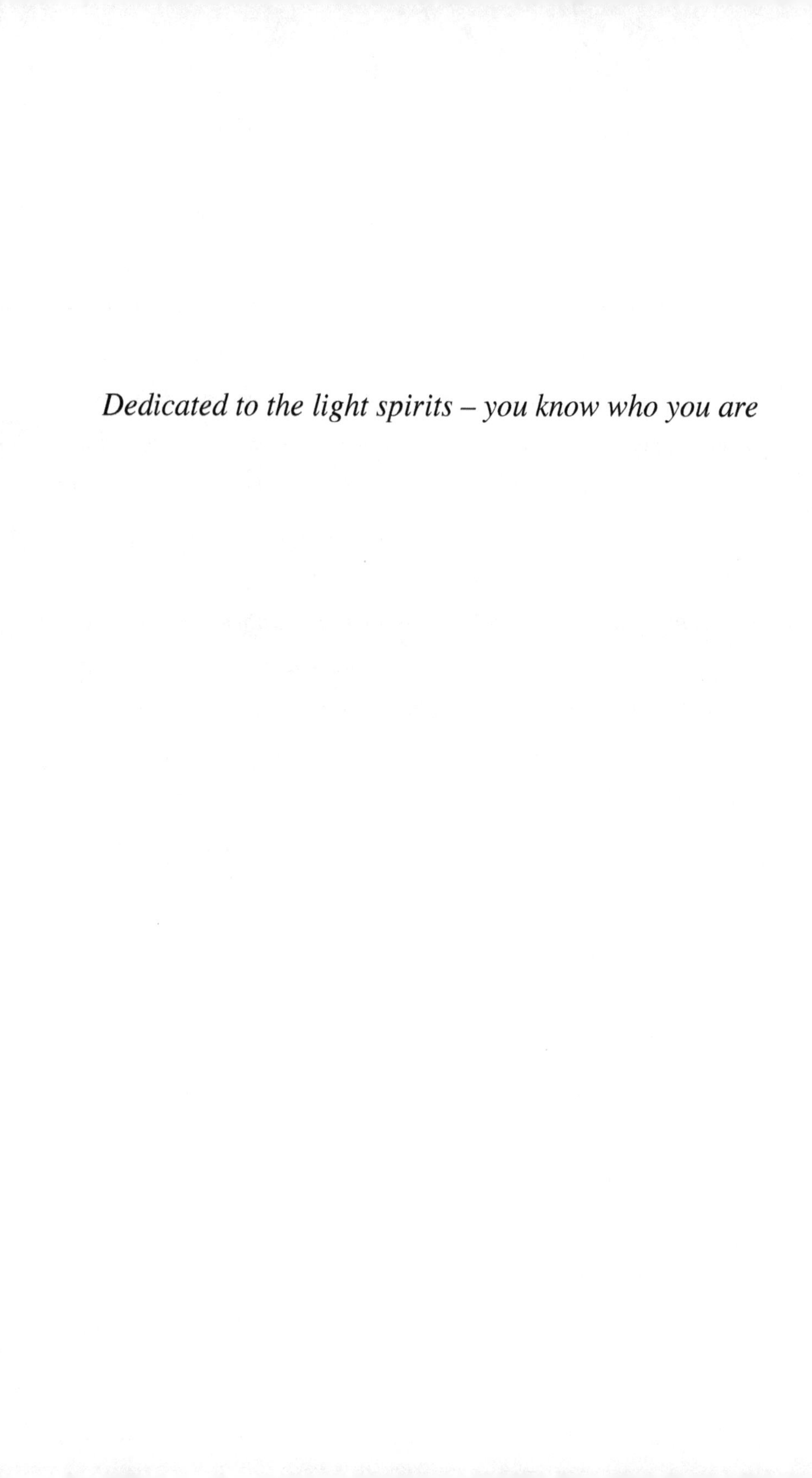

Dedicated to the light spirits – you know who you are

Chapter One

If clarity is never achieved

Then nothing has been gained

Tune Reference: *On A Clear Day*

----Alan Jay Lerner and Burton Lane

ON ONE CLEAR, very clear summer's day in Wichita Falls, Texas, a group of twelve year old girls in racing swimsuits gathered at the edge of a crystal blue twenty-five meter pool.

"Swimmers take your mark," barked the man behind the megaphone. He stood along the side of the swimming pool which faced Carrie. The shimmering water at her feet mirrored the reflection of the cloudless sky above.

Eight ten year old girls who had been anxiously standing at the edge of the pool curled into starting position. Each reached firmly for the bottom of the clock with every muscle cocked for the firing of the pistol.

The man holding the megaphone pointed his pistol upward and abruptly fired into the air.

Go! Carrie silently echoed as her legs automatically unfolded. Her arms embraced the entire distance of the body of water awaiting her. She gently greeted the water with a series of swift arm pulls and dolphin kicks.

Good. The water is warm, she thought, registering the temperature internally. Although extensive practice caused her to react as a finely tuned machine, she still registered the shock of cold water. Keeping her life simple, she relied on her body to win the race, while allowing her psyche to provide the drive and determination.

Her body released tension with the buoyant feeling and the ease of movement. Like an aqueous friend, the water felt alive and rejuvenated her senses. She kicked and pulled her way through the sparkling blue liquid like a newborn emerging into a another world.

Time stood still for a few seconds while all movement became slow motion. Carrie felt her body glide over the water like a hydrofoil. Everything moved according to its own rhythm: people followed biorhythms, planets twirled on their axes at predictable rates, and light bounced in a pattern prescribed by its color. The universe became a ballet of diversified participants, all dancing to their own beat, while remaining consistent with the universal pattern. Somehow for the present she managed to match her form to the relative rhythm of the liquid. The water and Carrie assumed the same wavelength as her body skimmed the surface without ever seeming to touch the pool beneath her.

She opened her eyes and surveyed the unbroken blue ahead of her. Although she remained in the lead, her position in the race no longer mattered. As spellbound as Icarus by the idea of flight, she became absorbed by the sensation of swimming. Sometime within the same minute, she fell back down to earth. Carrie became conscious of the cheering spectators and her arms began to feel heavy.

Spirit is willing but flesh is weak, Carrie mused as she adjusted her stroke to compensate for tiring muscles. She took a deep breath, closed her eyes, and thrust her head into the water.

Her arms rapidly circled over the water two more times. Squinting through the splashes, she estimated the remaining distance before the finish.

More strokes. More kicks. Only three more strokes until the end of the pool! Holding her breath she fought her way through the waves. Time to give it all...No more joyriding...Her circling arms stretched for the wall and finished the race.

She gently floated on her back, allowing the water to support her body. Then Carrie returned to the end of the pool and lifted her weary body out of the water. Turning to face the clock, she connected with the reality of her efforts. The moment of reckoning had arrived. Had she been as fast as she had imagined? Had she actually beat the clock?

"Looking good!" Coach Gramm yelled. He stood among the crowds surrounding the pool.

Carrie quietly nodded, as if bringing his words into her heart. A firm, but easygoing coach, he never placing any undue pressure on a young swimmer to compete. He represented one of the few coaches she knew who fostered a true enjoyment of the sport in his swimmers. Some coaches resorted to intimidation and peer pressure to squeeze faster times out of their swimmers, but Coach Gramm challenged his swimmers while they were relaxed and not even thinking about competing. This enabled swimmers to concentrate on their own ability to achieve success, rather than rely on external sources for motivation. Carrie smiled back at Coach Gramm before glancing at the times posted behind the starting blocks. She beamed at the results, her fastest race ever! Her feelings concerning the event matched her time. Much had occurred within a minute and a half. Recalling the peace that she had enjoyed while gliding over the water, Carrie savored the experience of a clear day vision. She found resonance with the water, harboring the same body, mind, and spirit. A fast time could always be faster and won by someone else, but the memory of the event remained hers to keep. That clear day underneath the scorching life, giving her a sense of belonging in the universe. The impression gleaned from this hot summer's day would help her remember her place and what she wanted out of life during the dark storms of confusion and self doubt.

Chapter Two

Some people find that
They have no choice

Tune Reference: *Bless The Beasts And The Children*
----Barry Vorzon and Perry Botkin, Jr.

LONG BEFORE THE experience during the swim meet, the Nightmare haunted Carrie. As far back as she could see, she had always lived with it. This Nightmare had many forms and it appeared at significant turning points throughout her life. The forms mirrored the way Carrie's world had changed, reminding her of a link to something dark and ominous in her past. Sometimes she knew this mirror as oblivion, sometimes as darkness, and sometimes as a light so white and bright that it hurt her eyes to see. Whenever this Nightmare occurred, all of Carrie's senses were annihilated, obliterating her perception of the present and coldly leaving her for the world of the dead.

In spite of its threat, this Nightmare made Carrie feel very sane because the Nightmare recognized her real feelings about the present. The Nightmare exposed her deepest thoughts, revealing their significance in her life. Nobody seemed to understand Carrie like this Nightmare; it told her the things that she should know about herself and the world. She never understood why it terrorized her. She never could see any motive behind the Nightmare. She could not ignore its existence, resenting the paralyzing effect on her senses. After the watching the Nightmare play out, she'd greet the day with a renewed sense of vitality and a vow to overcome the previous night's shock. The Nightmare represented some sort of judgement imposed on her. Finding it difficult to articulate, she sensed that nobody seemed to have the capacity to realize its meaning. She eventually concluded that she had not been the cause of such darkness.

One of the most vivid manifestations of the Nightmare occurred when Carrie became seven years old. During this time period in her life, Carrie lived in a brown stucco house located about a half-mile away from the Los Angeles International Airport. In this house Carrie shared a bedroom with Ellen, her younger sister by one and one-half years. A braided oval rug in the middle of walls were painted in turquoise. Despite being located next to the closet door, Carrie liked being as far away from Ellen as possible. Ellen always tore the heads off the dolls she played with and left their twisted naked bodies lying on the floor in front of her bed. She made the community of dolls look as if godzilla had visited them.

One day Carrie had arrived home from school and found her doll lying face down among the stark bodies. Wincing at the sight, she expressed her sorrow that she had not been wise enough to hide the doll from Ellen's grasp. Only two others remained untouched by Ellen, Carrie's male doll and the life-like baby doll sitting on the dresser between the window and Ellen's bed. The male doll stayed safe in his case underneath her bed.

After checking underneath her bed for the sight of his doll case, Carrie walked over to where the baby doll sat and examined it. Located in the section of the room that Carrie had let Ellen take over, its position on the dresser remained too high for Ellen's reach. This doll looked like a real live baby; Ellen didn't like it very much and never tried to reach it. Carrie searched the doll's face for any sign of expression over the hideous play which the doll had witnessed while she attended school. The doll seemed so life-like to Carrie that she still could not decide whether this baby was really a boy or a girl. Being just a baby, she couldn't tell. Carrie lightly ran her fingers across the doll's face and tried to close the eyes. The painted eyes would not close. Then she touched the doll's forearm, letting her fingers trace down the skin and fall into the doll's little hands. The doll felt hard and cold to Carrie. She always cared for the doll as best she could without being obvious. If she showed that she liked it, then Ellen might cry for it and her parents would make her give the doll to her younger sister. The gesture would silence Ellen and that would be the end of her nice doll.

After Carrie straightened the doll's light blue dress, she went over to the closet near her bed. Carrie opened the door and sat down in the darkness. Clothes hung all around her and the small closet barely had enough room for her. She had to move aside a few boxes to make herself comfortable. Ellen had taken over most of the bedroom for her activities and things, while Carrie had retreated to the closet for a safe place. Carrie knew that Ellen would not follow her there because Ellen voiced fears of the dark.

Gazing at the arrangement in the closet, a wonderful idea sparked her imagination. She decided to become an astronaut and make the closet her spaceship. For the next few days Carrie concerned herself with the project of converting the closet into a space capsule. She created an instrument panel with a chalkboard and colored chalk. The chalkboard served as the viewing screen, while Carrie drew in her destinations to all the various planets as she traveled through the galaxies. She simulated space travel by closing the closet door and turning on a flashlight which illumined the instrument panel. Ellen became fascinated with Carrie's spaceship, forgetting the fear of the dark as she claimed her half of the closet. In order to avoid an argument, Carrie reluctantly let her younger sister into the spaceship and made Ellen promise not to report her to her mother. Ellen began cooperating with Carrie under the circumstances.

Eventually, the Nightmare interrupted Carrie's spaceship travels rather than Ellen's endeavors. The first Nightmare came after the family's visit to their friend's house. After enjoying a hike with friends in the foothills surrounding the city, they came across the body of a dead animal. The fathers in the group motioned for them to stop. Underneath a young tree laid the deteriorating carcass of a small lamb. Wisps of soft, wooly white hung on the quiet bones like cotton. Curiously Carrie studied the animal skeleton in the yellowed blades of grass, and saw nothing frightening about the appearance of death. Tucked quietly in the oak in peace and she never would have seen it without the aid of the other people on the hike.

"Probably died because it strayed from the pack," Carrie's father remarked in a threatening voice. He looked directly at her.

Evading his glance, she shrugged and stepped back and closed herself within the ranks of the rest of the hiking group.

"Yes, it probably was lost and a wolf or some other wild animal killed it," the other father said, gazing sorrowfully at the dead lamb. He knelt on one knee as if to pay his last respects. A painful thought flickered across his countenance and he immediately rose. Fearing the separation associated with death, he discreetly pulled his children safely towards him with his eyes.

"Let's head back now. It's getting dark," he announced with his hands protectively on his children's shoulders.

Together they hiked in an invisible subgroup with Carrie's father being the only stray. Her friend's father smiled at her as Carrie followed alongside his family. He seemed to understand her choice. Feeling temporary relief from her father's words, Carrie happily noticed Ellen following close behind her. The hikers returned to the familiar ground of suburbia just before the sun sank behind the hills. The lights of the neighborhood twinkled cheerfully in the twilight and welcomed them to civilization. Gazing back at the distant hillside one last moment after the trek ended, Carrie discovered something that still concerned her. The experience of finding the dead lamb didn't bother her; death danced to the natural rhythm of life and music of the hills. Her father's misplaced accusations silently echoed in the hills. She really didn't understand his malice towards her. Separating her father's actions from the rest of the hike, Carrie fondly remembered her time on the hillside.

Two days after the visit to her friend's house, she began having a nightmare connecting the dead lamb, a human skeleton, and her closet. The closet contained a hidden passage connecting a skeleton to the site where the dead lamb had been found, and this skeleton threatened to wrap Carrie in its bony embrace. Tonight someone had left the closet door open before turning out the bedroom lights. Carrie froze in bed as the skeleton came to see her. When the skeleton seized her, she felt no more. She tried to escape, but she could not move. Repulsed by the icy touch, she stared into the hollow black eyes. The skeleton laughed as she wrestled to escape. Closing her eyes, Carrie attempted making the skeleton go away in her mind. She wanted to sleep, but it would not leave her in peace. She could not stop it; she could still feel the blackness creeping its way out of the closet towards her. Her mother would reprimand her if she got out of bed. Silent tears rolled down her face as she succumbed to the terror.

A sharp blow from out of nowhere struck her across the forehead, pinning her body to the bed. The blow caused her to regain her senses. Carrie opened her eyes and peered at the darkness left in the room. Sinking back into their cavity underneath the strain of another sleepless night, her eyes weighted her head like a couple of stones. She didn't want to see anymore. In the vague dark mirror of her room Carrie saw that she had begun to resemble the hollowed out skeleton. Immediately, the skeleton departed from her bed, leaving her to take its place amongst the greenish-blue walls of her room.

Boom! Crunch! The mildewed wall next to her bed seem to crash down on her, breaking her spirit, destroying everything nice until the deathly smell of the collapse permeated her life's breath. The crash left nothing untouched, permeating all of her being.

.   She stayed in bed and silently waited for the first rays of sunlight to appear around the shaded window. Still shivering from the cold of the dark night, Carrie remained frozen in the devastation. Although she had no power over her motionless body, she could see. She let her eyes move for her and take in the room's former appearance. Carrie saw that she did not like the room. She felt no attachment for her world; nothing in it that moved her or could bring her back from the world of the sleepless dead.

More light entered the room as the wee hours in the morning steadily passed. Carrie's world awoke from the darkness, and she tried wiggling her toes underneath the blankets. Yes, she could still feel life there, relieved that her mother never noticed that she had quit wearing socks to bed. Her mother always wanted her to cover them, though Carrie enjoyed experiencing the world through her feet.

Bounce! Bounce! Squeak! Squeak! Now she could hear her baby sister Samantha moving around in her crib in the room next door. Soon Carrie's mother would turn on the light in their bedroom and tell them to get ready for school.

When Carrie's mother had flipped on the light in the bedroom, Carrie hopped out of bed and retrieved her school uniform from the closet. Using the power of daylight to her own advantage, she carefully examined the contents of her closet and looked for the skeleton's secret passageway. She realized that she played a game called hide-and-go seek with the Nightmare.

Chapter Three

Take heart that some things
Can be left for yesterday

Tune Reference: *Yesterday*
----John Lennon and Paul McCartney

FOR THE NEXT few weeks Carrie made sure that the closet door remained closed before the lights were turned out at night. In spite of these precautions, there came one night when Carrie forgot to check. This time somebody had left the closet door opened six inches instead of three. As a result, the skeleton arrived at her bed even faster than the previous night. Carrie wanted to quickly close the opening, but feared being caught by her mother for getting out of bed.

As soon as the skeleton reached her, Carrie felt it inflict blow upon blow. In her dream, Carrie saw her mother's thick wooden brush, the stick that she used for punishment. Carrie wished that the stick would break so that her mother would be forced to discard it. She hated being hit on the head. The feeling of her mother maliciously hurting her that bothered her most of all. Years ago, about the age of five, she stayed up all night crying over her mother, who would punish her and put her to bed for reasons that she never understood. She yearned to talk to her mother and hoped that she would return to make peace. Her mother never came, and Carrie's hot tears turned to soft whimpers in the night.

Almost a year later, Carrie found her words and confronted her mother during a verbal joust in the kitchen. "I'm running away."

Her mother continued to toy with her. "Good."

Then she left the kitchen and left Carrie to pack some food for the journey. She filled a paper sack with peanut butter ritz cracker sandwiches and caught Ellen's attention. After Ellen packed her own sack, they climbed the five foot white picket fence to unleash the latch on the gate. The gate swung open and they walked out. The neighbors on the corner asked them where they were going. They replied that they were running away.

After rounding the corner up the hill, darkness began to settle on the subdivision. Carrie spied her mother and father walking towards them with their family dog Fluffy. Her shoulders dropped with disappoint that her were only two houses down the street. With an air of resignation, Carrie and Ellen silently trudged back home behind them.

Tonight she fell prey to the black hollowness inside the skeleton's eyes, where she died in their depths. The feeling broke Carrie, shattering her heart. When the skeleton disappeared, Carrie wept for her mother. In her pain she obediently remained in bed.

I'm seven years old, she quietly told herself one day. She sensed that something had change, as scar tissue had formed over the wound in her heart. Confronting the world with cool intellect, she left the world of imagination and make-believe, which no longer entertained her thoughts these days. Ready to move beyond her experiences, Carrie bravely looked at the opened closet again. She recalled the beautiful Blue fairy from the story Pinocchio. The kind Blue fairy told the wooden boy that she could help grant his wish to become a real boy. Somewhere in her depths Carrie felt the compassion of the Blue fairy stirring inside her. Reaching for her twirling baton below her bed, she managed to pick it up without ever stepping on the floor. The blackness of the night muted the brilliant color of her shiny blue baton. Carrie hid it under her blankets. Now she had her own stick, a magic wand or sword that would serve her. Carrie waited a few seconds before making her move with the baton. While listening cautiously to her mother's movements inside the house, Carrie slowly retrieved the baton from the blankets. Her mother would only be able to hear her from the living room. Luckily, from the sound of her mother's footsteps in the house, Carrie could tell that her mother sat in the kitchen now and well out of hearing distance for Carrie's bedroom. Without making any sounds she extended the length of the baton to the closet and pushed the door shut.

Carrie sighed with relief. *Won't get out this night.*

Armed with her shiny blue baton, Carrie fought her paralyzing fear and pushed back on the skeleton. Acting less like a puppet-child and more like a real person, she could change her predicament. She rolled out of bed and ventured cautiously from her bedroom. She found her mother sitting in the nearby living room, while her father stayed away for the evening. Entranced by the late night movie on television, she scarcely acknowledged Carrie's presence when she wandered into the room.

"Can't sleep," Carrie murmured, quickly mimicking her mother's stare at the television screen.

"It's a good movie," her mother replied, breaking from her normal response. Appreciating the company, she made no motion for Carrie to return to the bedroom. Relieved to be out of the darkness, Carrie relaxed the tension in her shoulders and took a few breaths. Somehow she had managed to break free from the skeleton's puppet dance.

"Time for bed," the mother announced, turning off the set when the show ended.

Carrie rose slowly from her place on the carpet. For one brief shining moment, she had broken the pattern of abuse. Her experience with the other father and the dead lamb had moved her. She found that the reality of death haunted her relationship with her parents, after attaining a world where parents didn't allow skeletons to grow in their kids closets. She glimpsed a place where relationships became more than just structure; parents protected their children out of concern rather than duty. The Nightmare had lost some of its potency and she didn't feel so scared anymore. The wound inside her heart could heal, though it might demand sacrificing her childhood.

The next morning Carrie rose from her bed, retrieved her clothes from the closet, and ran to the door between the living room and her sister's bedroom. Before dressing in her baby sister's room Carrie always peered inside to make sure Samantha wasn't asleep. Sure enough, her one and a half year old sister already bounced in her crib. She smiled at Carrie when she spied her older sister through the slight opening in the door.

"Jeepers! Creepers! Where did you get them peepers!" Carrie sang as she burst into the room. She ran to Samantha, rubbing noses with her until both blue eyes were level with the other sister's, and dramatically ended her song: "...where did you get those EYES!"

Samantha laughed and rubbed her tiny hands together, as Carrie loved danced around her. Reveling in the baby's smile and cheerful atmosphere, Carrie expressed admiration for Samantha's readiness and entertained her with toys. Dressing by the heater as opposed to the coldness of her own room, Carrie continued to hold her sister's attention with her words, "Good morning, peeper! How's the peeper doing today? What's Sam up to?"

Understanding the dangers of being mistaken for a live doll, Carrie readily adopted her mother's nickname for the baby as her own term of affection. Rather than fuss over the blonde, blue-eyed little girl, Carrie preferred to play with her.

"Jeepers, creepers, where d'ja get 'em peepers!" Carrie cooed as she placed her baton safely on the floor. She paraded several stuffed animals past the baby.

Meanwhile, Samantha leaned on the crib rail and bounced in time to the music, becoming more animated when Carrie started singing and dancing crib until one particular toy reached Samantha's eager grasps. "This little chick with the soft yellow fur reminds me of Samantha most of all. You're the chick with the yellow fuzz on top," Carrie smiled at Samantha. All her sisters had blond hair and blue eyes like their father.

Samantha caught the tiny chick in her arms and drew the stuffed toy towards her gracefully as her awkward limbs would fly around the object. Once she had encircled the soft toy, she cooed and giggled at it.

"It goes "peep, peep,"" Carrie corrected her. "All little chicks go "peep, peep" at the world when they break through their eggs."

Thump! Samantha threw her chick on the floor below her crib. Then she leaned far over the edge to inspect the results. She leaned so far towards the ground that Carrie became alarmed that she might tumble out after the bird.

"What? You want someone to pick up your chick for you? OK, Sammy Peeper, I'll show you how to pick up chicks!" Carrie announced. Then she quickly bent over the chick, so that Samantha would stay in her crib. Curious, Samantha watched her closely. When Carrie handed her the bird, she tossed it across the room again. Noticing how Samantha's eyes followed the toy after it landed, Carrie voiced sorrow for her sister's confinement. "You're only peepin' at the world," Carrie observed. She picked up the bird and danced the chick in front of Samantha's reach. The ruse worked. The dancing motion of the small yellow bird captivated the infant's attention. Samantha tightly grasped the bird by its yellow fur and brought it to her opened mouth. Slobbering over the stuffed toy, she sat down inside the crib. Carrie happily watched how much the little chick absorbed Samantha's attention. Satisfied that she wouldn't have to play *pick up the chick* again, Carrie left the room to finish getting ready for school.

Chapter Four

Sometimes you don't

Need to go far to

Find the truth

Tune Reference: *Sunny*

----Bobby Hebb

ALTHOUGH THE NIGHTMARE persisted well into Carrie's adult years, there were other memories of her youth that guided her through life. These cherished gems of unique experiences shined through life's storms and gently reminded her to trust whatever seemed to come her way. She used these precious moments to restore her clarity and perspective. Usually there was something in her own nature that helped her identify these gems, because their discovery depended on her own prospecting.

Carrie found one such gem at the very young age of five years. She enjoyed being with a playmate named Kenny who lived across the street. Being one year older than Carrie, Kenny seemed much more worldly. He often brought a welcomed sophistication to their child's play.

"Wanna try a puff?" he asked her one day.

Admiring Kenny's latest prop, Carrie watched him elegantly smoke a cigarette on the end of a long holder. "No thank you," she decided, refusing to test her mother's eyesight from the living room window.

Keeny nodded his understanding and continued to smoke alone. Because they always played very well together, his mother sincerely believed that they would marry each other when they became older. Sometimes Kenny would walk with her to school and show her where he had his first grade class. When the other boys called her "Kenny's girlfriend," Kenny only smiled and firmed his grip on their interlocking hands.

As one of the their favorite games became "Batman and Robin," Kenny and Carrie unconsciously stayed in these characters throughout their relationship. Even when playing doctors, they still kept their hidden identity as Batman and Robin. Kenny played the role of Batman, whereas Carrie played his partner Robin. Being a girl, they created a different Robin; their Robin portrayed woman just as wise and capable as Batman. She became Batman's companion rather than the ward of a wealthy guardian. Though Kenny and Carrie played many other games such as cowboys and indians, pirates, army, and doctors, their favorite game proved "Batman and Robin." Kenny possessed a clever imagination and artistic sense that flourished in his repertoire of costumes and props. They both relished making their play as realistic as possible. Wearing his black Batman cape, Kenny often cruised in Carrie's driveway with the announcement: "Let's go, Robin!" Quickly she'd hop on his bike and they would zip down the sidewalk in caped crusader fashion.

One day during a game of army doctors, Kenny proposed the idea of listening to Carrie's breathing with his stethoscope. He wanted to be just like a doctor, and one of the most important activities of being a doctor involved hearing a person breathe. Carrie eagerly nodded her head at Kenny's fun idea of being a doctor. As soon as she had given her consent, he asked, "OK if I undo the buttons that are on the back of your shirt?"

"OK," she told him.

"I'll be careful," Kenny assured her.

They were as quiet as a city without an airport. Carrie felt Kenny's unbutton the top button. "Breathe deeply," he whispered softly. His fingers felt warm on the back of her neck. She took her deepest breath and slowly released it.

"Again," he quietly demanded while listening through his stethoscope.

Being so close to her, she could hear Kenny's breathing as well as her own. Determined to be a real doctor, he directed his curiosity in a very professional manner. Releasing only the top three of her buttons on the back of her blouse, his examination remained gentle and deliberate. Carrie felt touched by the amount of care and concern Kenny demonstrated, treating her as if a prized jewel.

Kenny took off his shirt when Carrie's turn came to be doctor. He looked very handsome and she earnestly wanted to treat him as wonderfully as he had cared for her. She tried to be as delicate in her touch as possible while still exhibiting the same degree of skill as he had done. Noticing his smooth tan body go limp with the motion of her hands, Carrie observed the effect she desired. She felt very pleased and proud that he enjoyed her efforts.

As if by magic, her perception of her environment changed at that moment. Looking across the backyard, Carrie watched the crystal dew drops dance underneath the sun's warmth on the green grass. The skin on her forearms tingled with the air's fresh spirit as she heard the birds sing their morning songs like a dozen tiny bells echoing through the atmosphere. Immediately she became conscious of another part of her existence, of life and death, the freedom and tranquility associated with nature. Moving outside their childlike existence, they discovered that they were not alone; they had heard the breath of life.

Carrie stopped as they both listened to the music in the air surrounding them. Resuming their play of army doctors, they seemed intent on preserving life in a war that they could only feel but not see. It was the mid-sixties and there had been adult whispers of revolutions going on in the world. They had found something very real in their game of make-believe. When the time came for Kenny to return to his home across the street, they smiled as two good friends and waved their goodbyes. Both had been deeply touched by the experience and left with the sensation of having peered across the threshold at some wonderful secret concerning man and woman. They never played doctors again. The play seemed too trivial for what they had felt. Like Batman and Robin, they never ventured into any encounter where they weren't prepared.

Chapter Five

Be wary of whatever happens too fast

Tune Reference: *All I Know*

----Art Garfunkel

AFTER CARRIE'S EIGHTH birthday, the family moved to a small town in Texas. The scenery changed from hippies, peace signs, psychedelic murals along the beach to craven cowboys, Jesus Saves signs, and herds of slow grazing cattle. In Los Angeles, Carrie had spent entire recesses with her friends pretending that they were horses and would run to avoid being captured and tamed. The rugged Southwest terrain suited her taste for the wild as well as her adventurous spirit. The boys called her "speedy" because she could run faster than any of them. Carrie relished being a maverick on the plains and excelled in her academic pursuits as well. The years passed quickly and soon she entered high school.

During the early autumn of her sophomore year in high school, Carrie's class decided to construct a class float for the homecoming parade. The high school totaled approximately 2800 students, divided into three rival classes; Sophomores, Juniors, and Seniors. Of the three, the Sophomore class seemed the largest and the most disorganized, a condition which made class projects impossible. Their youth and lack of experience earned them campus ridicule, which undermined their class spirit even further. As a result, Carrie's class, developed within itself a cocky sense of pride in order to get the job done.

"Hey, Mike we need some more tissue paper over here!" Shelly yelled. She served as leader of the section where Carrie worked, and had previous experience in float construction.

"Come-ing!" Mike hollered as he hurried off to retrieve more sheets of paper. "That section looks re-al good," he told a busy group of assembly line workers.

"Gosh, it sure is nice of Margaret's parents to donate their driveway for this Sophomore class float," Shelly observed as she stopped her task for the moment and surveyed the rest of the operation.

"Yes, they won't be able to use it for the next month. The Sophomore float for Edison High School is being constructed next door to my house. They have students working in their backyard twenty-fours a day," Carrie commented.

"What! You live in Edison territory!" Shelly exclaimed.

"Only a block away from the school," Carrie acknowledged, biting her lip as she recalled the bitter rivalry between Edison and her chosen school. "I wanted to be on the swim team, so I transferred school districts. Edison doesn't have a pool for a swim team," she explained. Many of Carrie's friends on the team were transfer students, people that she had known them since ten years old. Fortunately, most of the neighbors in her block respected her desire to excel in swimming and overlooked the rivalry. Carrie had attended the local school the previous year and had earned their friendship.

Mike arrived with more paper to fill in the holes of the chicken mesh. The float would consist of a series of wire section which fitted a design. Each hole in the wire section had to be filled with color paper according to the overall pattern.

"We're going to be one of the first Sophomore classes to win the float competition," Mike promised. "I heard that the Junior's float is three-quarters finished and looks pretty crummy."

"Well, things are moving pretty slow here," Shelly said with a sigh.

"Maybe we should start working twenty-four hours like Edison's Sophomore class," someone suggested.

"We should have someone guard it too. Some of Edison's seniors are threatening to burn the Junior's float. A few Juniors from our school stole their spirit stick. Somehow they managed to lift it from the school office and walk off campus with it," Mark said with a hint of worry in his voice. Although a spirit stick simply consisted of a baton painted with the school's colors, it symbolized the high school's honor. As a coveted possession, the baton went to the class which demonstrated the most spirit at the weekly pep rallies.

"Ya, we can't expect Margaret and her family to stay at home all the time," Carrie added.

"We could have a major gang war on our hands," Shelly frowned. As class president, one of her duties consisted of representing the Sophomores as a group of civilized students.

"Let me know what is decided," Carrie told Shelly. "My father is supposed to pick me up at eight o'clock and I must go now...See ya tomorrow!" Carrie waved at the group. Then she walked down the long driveway to the street's curb and waited.

Her father never came, though it was not unusual for Carrie's parents arrive an hour or two late. She sat on the curb, waiting in the darkness, while her classmates waved good-by and went home. The owner of the house came and asked her if she needed to call her parents. Carrie shook her head in response and moved away from the house. Squinting at the empty roads, she deliberated whether to walk home and pass a place where teenagers had been found hanging in an old graveyard.

"Get in!" Her mother shouted as she drove up beside Carrie and opened the passenger door. Carrie had only made it halfway up the block before her mother's arrival. "Why didn't you call?" her mother angrily continued.

"Dad agreed to pick me up," she reminded her. Her mother knew of Carrie's arrangements, having set them up herself. She planned to arrive home after ten, when her class finished.

Her mother drove a block down the street and stopped at a four way stop sign. Suddenly her father's car emerged from the street to their right. He turned and stopped alongside her mother's car. Opening his car door as if to rescue her from her mother, he calmly said, "Get in, Carrie."

Carrie didn't move. She didn't trust her father either, and his words and actions seemed strangely inappropriate considering the circumstances. Carrie's mother quieted. As soon as his attention focused on his wife, Carrie quickly locked her door so that he would not be able to pull her from the car if he became angry.

"I'm picking her up," her mother told him. Her mother and father argued feebly for a few minutes, while the time passed like hours for Carrie. Then her mother drove away and her father followed a few blocks behind them.

"He's been out this whole time. You should have called me. He has probably been drinking," her mother yelled at Carrie as she accelerated down the familiar streets towards home. "There are too many things going on at home. See what happened tonight!"

I wish she had told me before I made plans to attend the gathering, Carrie thought as she wistfully stared at the calm blackness of the sleeping neighborhoods. Puzzled by the sudden change in her situation and dramatic contrast with the quiet environment, she focused on her immediate surroundings and numbly gazed at the glovebox. Then she shook her head and looked helplessly out the passenger window.

After parking the car in the driveway, she continued talking while Carrie quietly walked through the front door. Carrie ignored her and marched towards the room she shared with Samantha, She left Carrie in the darkness and hurried to her own room without anymore verbal assaults. Once Carrie heard the cold click of her mother's bedroom lock, she sighed with relief. Safe from her mother's harangue, she rested in bed. Soon Carrie's father arrived and turned off all the lights in the house. He slept in the living room.

In the quiet black comfort of the night, Carrie cried. Like a swimmer caught in a fast moving river, she could not get out of the current events which seem to direct her life, unable to defend herself even verbally with her mother. Something about her parents trapped her and killed her inside. She didn't know how to explain herself in such a hopeless, fearful situation. Nobody listened. Her parents reminded her of the Nightmare. Tonight, Carrie knew the Nightmare in a different form. Staring at her from the darkness of confusion, she saw the face of death accusing her. Driving under the influence of many demons, her father might take them both out in a car wreck. She wanted to be free from the Nightmare's coldness, but she could see no other options before her.

Carrie felt more tears roll down her cheek. Whatever trapped her also had the power to kill her. Realizing that her emotions concerning the Nightmare were lethal, she decided to cut them off before she gave into them. Was the Nightmare really her fault? Carrie would die if she was to blame. Why bother trying to survive with the Nightmare?

Somewhere in the back of Carrie's subconscious stirred the memory of a teenage boy who once lived at the far end of her block. He had included Carrie in one of the neighborhood baseball games at a crucial moment during her early teen years. Although Carrie was about four years younger than the rest of the players, she loved playing ball and welcomed any opportunity to block, because she attended a different school, perpetually considered the new kid on the block.

While the older kids busily organized the teams, Carrie observed the chaos from the curb. She didn't want to commit to their aggressive antics. Besides being rather reserved, she disagreed with about seventy-five percent of the capers that most of the older kids pulled, and she wanted to play ball without getting involved in their delinquency.

Everyone waited for a fellow by the name of Brian to join the group as if they couldn't play without him. Evidently Brian possessed some special quality that captivated the attention and respect of even the roughest bullies.

"Where's Brian?" someone asked.

"Go get Brian!" another commanded.

"Will Brian play?" they questioned.

Brian piqued Carrie's curiosity. What did people see in him? She studied Brian as he exited the house at her right. He casually strolled across the grassy front lawn in his bare feet and greeted his friends waiting on the street. He appeared to be carrying a slight weight on his shoulders and his clothes hung on his delicate athletic form. When he saw the gang of players eager for coed baseball, his face immediately brightened. It was his desire to be with people rather than his enthusiasm for the sport that had lured him away from his bedroom sanctuary. His eyes surveyed the appearance of every individual in the group as if he held a personal interest in their wellbeing. No one seem to be aware of his gaze. Content with having won him as their prize, the teams ignored his presence and continued their frolic. Nonetheless, Brian held silent leadership status in the group, and no definite decisions were made without his consultation.

Maintaining a slight distance from the rest, Carrie stood almost directly to his right and pondered the social game. When he turned towards her, Carrie met his gaze. He smiled at the her and instinctively puffed out his chest proudly. Swept by his gesture, she returned his smile and instantly fought the compulsion to turn her head away. Carrie preferred meeting males on equal ground, no matter how cute they seemed. Of all the boys that she had ever played baseball with, Brian had been the first to acknowledge her feminine attributes rather than her baseball skills. Her heart immediately soared to her head. She flew over to the team that selected her as if Brian, himself, had drawn her closer under his wing.

After the baseball game, Brian and Carrie went their different directions. The five year age difference discouraged a relationship. Carrie contented herself with being an admirer. The following year Brian went away to study at a university four hours from his home. Sometime during the next spring Brian fell to his death from the heights of the university stadium. The local newspapers headlined the controversy surrounding his death.

Never bothering to read the newspaper articles herself, Carrie heard enough about the story from her parent's conversations. Although the medical examiner ruled his death a suicide, some of his family and close friends vehemently protested, claiming that the physicians victimized the young man. For several years, Brian had undergone drug therapy for depression without any positive results. Those who knew him insisted that the prescribed drugs destroyed his perception of reality and emotional balance, causing him to fall unintentionally during a confused state.

Since many of the family's relatives lived by the college where the young man had died, they held the funeral in the same city. Relations planned a memorial service at the parish church a few days after the funeral. Since the young man's parents were nonpracticing parishioners, the priest seized the opportunity to bring the family back into the fold. He counseled the parents during their grief, blaming Brian for his own tragedy and relieving the parent's guilt.

Carrie attended the memorial service to pay her respects. Only one other person besides herself and Brian's younger sister represented the kids from that day of the baseball game. Relieved that the casket ceremony had been held elsewhere, Carrie intended to remember Brian for the spirit she had known. Before the end of Mass, his younger sister approached the lectern and expressed the same intention.

"I want to remember Brian as I knew him. He always enjoyed playing his records in his room. There is one song that he loved to play all the time, it best describes the Brian that I knew." Then she left the podium before her tears choked her. Kneeling over the phonograph with a microphone attachment, she placed the needle on the revolving record.

The song *All I Know* by Art Garfunkel, embraced the entire congregation. Serving as Brian's self-defense for his own murder, the words and melody embodied Brian's spirit, the same spirit which sang with Art Garfunkel and pierced the hearts of those who listened.

Looking around the congregation, Carrie noticed that many people quietly rocking themselves with their tears. Those who cried understood Brian and his passionate struggle to create love in a world of pain. Like a young Icarus, he had dared to escape the circumstances of his existence and had flown too high in his quest, a pattern often characteristic of the desperate. Through his death he stirred the sleeping Daedalus inside those who also flew on the wings of love, and they awoke mourning for their lost son.

Her mother's friend, Grace, who came with them to the service also wept when she heard the song. During the drive home she recalled how Brian had helped her locate her missing child when he worked as an usher at the local movie theater.

"He seemed different than the rest. He cared enough to go out of his way and help me find my son. He understood my concern as a mother." Then she looked down at the floor of the car, shaking her head at the recognition of another son. People missed now. "There is something about our society that seems to kill those who are most beautiful and sensitive...the good die young," she continued, sobbing in frustration and grief.

"Yes, he was too good," Carrie's mother added sadistically while smiling at the clouds in the sky.

The memory Brian struck Carrie like icy cold water thrown across her face. Identifying with Brian's struggle in her own family, the Nightmare represented death for Carrie. People like her parents would have killed Brian just to get him to heaven sooner. What was the point of a life? With this revelation Carrie forgot her thoughts on suicide and suddenly remembered her low tolerance to pain, her queasy stomach, and the fact that she went into shock easily at the sight of there had been many people that she had known and loved. People like Grace lived compassionately in the world, as did others who were just as nice as the kids that she worked with on the Sophomore float. She vowed to make connections with the people that were unlike her parents; the ones who could feel for Brian and help him live. If only she could survive the despair of this night and see the dawn of a new day, then her spirit would rejuvenate with the sunrise.

With the intention of staying afloat in this crisis, Carrie inventoried the effects of her emotions on her body, as if in a swim race. She felt physically exhausted; in order to survive the next day, she required a good night's rest. Because the sinking portion of her feelings had to be left behind, a part of Carrie needed to die in the rebirthing process. These emotions were dragging her down and she needed to sever her ties from their weight or else perish in the depths. So she took three aspirin and committed an abbreviated version of hari-kari, reasoning that three aspirin would not kill her; nonetheless, she wanted to capitalize on the knockout effect. During the night, the portion of Carrie which had been formerly tied to the fate of her parents died.

The next morning, life resumed as usual without any reference to the stresses of the previous night. Carrie broke the silence at the breakfast table and confessed some of her feelings from the previous night to her mother. While Carrie cried, her mother told her that she'd surely go to hell if she ever considered acting on her feelings and ignored the present hellish situation. Carrie's father stood at the kitchen counter ready for work, numbly listening to their conversation as he slowly sipped his orange juice while staring out the window. Carrie didn't feel any better after talking with her parents.

She never worked on the class float again, and the project died after the float mysteriously burned to the ground a few weeks later, the arson target of either high school rivals or competing upper classmates. Concentrating on other flotation devices for self preservation, she buried herself in her studies as her only hope for an independent future. Carrie minimized her reliance on her parents and obtained a driver's license on the same day she became the legal age of sixteen. Using the license to provide dependable transportation for herself and sisters, Carrie judiciously limited contacts with friends to school hours. These temporary changes helped Carrie cope with her home situation.

Chapter Six

There's a lot to be said for humanity

Tune Reference: *People*

----Barbara Streisand and Bob Merrill

AS A TEENAGER, Carrie painfully buried the Nightmare in her subconscious. The feelings associated with it proved too deadly for further examination. However, bit by bit, she began the process of gathering information for herself that might help her unravel her tangled emotions. Often Carrie's best resources were the youngsters in her swimming classes.

"I don't wanna swim," the two-year-old boy cried. "There are sharks in the water," he concluded after scouting the chlorinated swimming pool.

Carrie studied the youth intently while thinking of a way to quiet his fears before he became hysterical. Once a two year old became fearful in situation, it became nearly impossible to deal with the main issue. Fear in a such a very young child had to be considered seriously, because it might permanently affect a child's attitude towards swimming. Two and three-year-old children generally took longer to recover from unpleasant experiences, much less make another attempt.

Carrie taught many children who had feared the water, and discovered that these fears usually affected self esteem and confidence in other areas of their lives. These students proved more challenging than others because an instructor confronted the psyche in addition to merely teaching a physical skill. As the psyche healed, the child became more assertive in the aqueous environment and swimming became fun.

From earlier lessons, Carrie had noticed how well the boy got along with other children his age. He possessed a certain type of charisma that enabled him to relate well with his peers. He did not appear to be a whiner, a brat, or a child with excessive anxiety. However, Carrie knew that he had something on his mind besides flutter kicking when he said on the first day in class, "My Daddy's up in heaven. My Mommy says that he's an angel."

Carrie listened to the boy's mimicked explanation of an event that he apparently had not fully grasped and remained quiet, not having anything to offer. After the lesson, a day care teacher confided to her that the boy's father had perished in a house fire earlier that spring.

Today, she stood waist high in the water trying to find the key which might release the youth from his feelings of entrapment. Apparently, swimming became a life or death issue for the lad. Unlike most children, he seemed very much aware of the sink or swim phenomena, and felt more attuned to the dangers of being physically attacked while swimming. She personally knew many adults who shared the same fears as the boy, especially after viewing the movie *Jaws* this year. Carrie felt that the boy had a legitimate concern. As a swimming instructor, she intentionally nurtured the consummate swimmer—someone who could swim comfortably under rough water conditions. Chlorinated swimming pools were just simulated models of oceanic and freshwater environments in which the chances of attacks were not remote. In freshwater a swimmer had to be alert for water moccasins and other poisonous snakes.

Besides the basic life and death question, vulnerability or the sense of being a powerless victim in a life threatening situation seemed another important issue. Recognizing the tragic loss of his parental guardian to circumstances beyond his own control, the youth realized his own vulnerability and demonstrated his refusal to involve himself in a situation that taxed his physical and psychological capacity. As she heard the boy's adamant stand from the nearby steps, Carrie couldn't help but admire his courage. This fellow's wisdom compensated for his puny external frame, as he proudly voiced concerns for his vulnerability.

She did too. She could recall her own experiences of vulnerability. Now Carrie faced the prospect of going away to college at the end of summer. Her parents had been separated for over a year now. Although the her to be a little bit apprehensive about making such a major change in her life.

Well, she asked herself, *what does one do when confronted by sharks in the water?* Carrie recalled a wildlife special that she had seen on T.V. about scuba diving and shark attacks.

"They say that the best way to beat a shark is to poke 'em in the eyes and hit them on the nose. Just pretend you are like one of the three stooges, make a peace sign with two of your fingers, and then jab the shark in the eyes like this," Carrie said as she punched an imaginary shark in the water to convince herself as well as the boy.

The youth picked up this skill in self-defense very quickly. "Like this!" he burst exuberantly while making peace signs at several imaginary underwater sharks.

"Yep, you've got the right idea," she answered, being careful not to encourage him too much. Instead she intentionally communicated several ideas to the boy: His fears were legitimate; he had the power within himself to cope with adversity and fear; and he had the right to protect himself and fight back.

The boy jumped excitedly off the steps, submerged his head underwater, and stabbed a few more pretend sharks. Having discovered a weapon he could safely rely on, he attempted a frontal glide complete with flutter kick. He kicked remarkably well for a two year old; the boy proved to be a natural swimmer.

Carrie sighed with relief, having freed the youth from his hopeless fear of sharks. Who knows when he would have ever entered the water again? She smiled to herself, grateful for discovering the key concept for the boy and having seen the T.V. special. Like other viewers, she had wondered what to do in case of a shark attack. The boy's enthusiastic response showed whatever attacked either of them would be pounded into hamburger meat.

Chapter Seven

The castles of our minds

Reflect our constructs

Tune Reference: *Teach Your Children*

----Crosby, Stills, and Nash

CARRIE BEGAN HER first year at a small liberal arts college, nestled deep in the wooded hills overlooking a nearby football stadium. The university remained cloistered from the affairs of the civilian world by location as well as ideology. A slogan spray painted on a campus water tower herald the university's philosophy: Home of the Fighting Phenomenologists. While walking on the wide brick mall that united the main buildings on campus, Carrie often felt as if she had entered another time zone. The founders of the university wished to create an old style European environment that contributed to the study of classical literature and art. Anachronistic in terms of architecture and core curriculum, the university ignored most literature following the eighteenth century with emphasis on Greek, Roman, and medieval studies.

Less than one month after the school year began, Carrie encountered a sophomore cross-country runner named Marty. Their relationship just sort of happened, or rather they mutually walked into each other's life as if there had been a space waiting for them. Carrie met Marty at one of the first dances held for start of the school year. On this warm summer night, Carrie stayed outside, away from the sea of unknown faces on the dance floor. She spent most of the evening chatting with her new college acquaintances outside on the veranda.

"Would you like to dance?" the tall, wiry man asked. He had a strawberry blond mane and could have easily passed as a Viking.

"Yes, I would," Carrie responded with a slight smile. For over an hour she had been amusing him with tales of her white water canoeing escapades, while Marty entertained her with stories describing the antics of the university cross country team. She had never spent so much time talking with one particular individual without stopping the conversation to throw a football or softball.

Marty and Carrie made their way through the crowd to the dance floor inside the glass building. Carrie could feel the strength of the drum beat vibrate inside her body and stole a quick look at Marty before giving way to the motion. Noticing how easily his eyes betrayed his emotions, she started to dance with his movements. There had been no ready defenses in their eager blueness, reflecting her same degree of inexperience. Carrie glanced at his face again to be sure of meaning in his expression. This time he met her gaze, allowing his body to sway to the music's time. His eyes danced with happy disbelief.

He likes you, Carrie, she thought to herself. Her heart moved with excitement. Everything about this guy seemed right for her. They danced together for the remainder of the evening, never leaving the dance floor until the band stopped playing and started to pick up their equipment. After the music stopped, Marty motioned Carrie to the veranda which offered a view of the sleeping city lights.

"So you and your roommate are going to drive cars for the rental agency tomorrow," he said with a big grin.

"Yeah, Richard is supposed to drop by in the morning," Carrie replied, eagerly looking forward to the new experience of driving for the car rental agency. The company hired university students to transfer cars between the many rental agencies scattered across the state. Carrie had met Richard earlier at the party. In addition to working for the car rental agency, Richard ran cross country and was Marty's good friend.

"My roommate Ernie is the one who handles the arrangements between the campus and the car rental agency. You'll meet him in the afternoon. He's going to pick up everyone who drives for tomorrow. …Ernie, he's an alright guy," Marty reflected, cocking his curly head to one side with his thoughts. "Sometimes I think he studies too hard and drinks too much, but he's one of those premed types. They all study hard and party hard. Most everyone here is like that." After pausing for a moment, he wryly observed, "I don't study near as much as the others. I have never been drunk to the point where I got sick or passed out. I have contro-o-ol," Then he moved towards her and softly asked, "So tell me about you..."

"Well, I am premed, but I believe that there is more to life than studying my brains out. I don't like beer and I have never been drunk to the point where I lost control or became sick," Carrie told him. "But I like to play hard," she teased, leaning forward to return his taunt.

Grinning from ear to ear, Marty reached for Carrie. Placing his arm around her waist he remarked, "You're just my type."

Suddenly realizing they were the only ones left on the veranda, the tone of their encounter grew serious.

"Mind if I walk you to your dorm. It's not so safe around here...there were a few incidents last year," he asked as he held Carrie's hand in concern. She felt his fingers tighten around her palm. They did not want to let go of her and told her more about Marty than anything else at the moment. She could feel his warmth. Carrie did not want to let go either.

"I would like that very much. I prefer to play it safe," she replied.

Marty firmly closed his hand around hers and led Carrie down the backstairs of the veranda. "Have you been by the Art department?" he asked. "There's a really nice walkway that goes through the woods. It goes directly to your dorm. People don't use it much, though. I guess they don't like walking through the woods. The university is full of the studious types that like to stick to the pavement."

Carrie looked beyond to the soft clay lights illuminating the path before her. Dark green vegetation cloaked the trail while moonlight glistened off the leaves, inviting Carrie to follow the swirling trail in front of her. "Yes, I like the woods and I haven't seen the Art department yet," she told him in almost a whisper.

They stepped on the white gravel covering the walkway. The softly lit path beckoned them to another world, a place where time followed the course of nature. Carrie quietly walked with Marty to an alcove hidden amongst the shadows. Leaving her one step higher than where he stood, he took both of her hands inside his. Then he softly kissed her lips.

Closing her eyes, Carrie returned his kiss. She could feel his heart racing against her breast. His gentle breath swept through her body like the wind. Parting from their embrace, they stood back for a few seconds. Marty's face shone with joy. Carrie trembled slightly with excitement. She could feel his radiance. Then she and Marty closed their eyes once more, melting into the warmth of the summer night with a soft kiss. In their fervent embrace she felt Marty's hands seek their way past her skin, gently lifting the clothing away. Cupping her into his hands, Marty tenderly caressed her with moist lips.

She sought him underneath the shimmering moonlight. In the whorl of feelings flooding her senses, Carrie unbuttoned Marty's shirt and explored his strong chest. Then their eyes met. She felt different as she began to see herself through his eyes. His sweet gaze swept over her as he closed his eyes, savoring his own heartbeat, while accepting the strength of his own vulnerability.

At two o'clock in the morning, Marty and Carrie said their good byes on the steps leading to the dormitory hallway. Since men were only permitted inside the building during certain hours on the weekend, they lingered on the stairs.

"What are you doing tomorrow night?" he asked as he kissed her.

They arranged to see each other the next evening before Carrie hurried to her dorm room. She expected to find her roommate already asleep in the room. However, a quick glance at her empty bed informed her that her roommate remained out for the evening.

Carrie awoke the next morning and dressed before Ernie picked her up to drive for the car rental agency. She had fallen asleep before her roommate's return last night. With similar lifestyles, no excuses would ever be necessary for staying out late. She looked in the mirror as she washed her face and thought about Marty and her feelings of the previous night. She had not even come close to crossing that threshold past virginity, finding fulfillment in simplicity. Marty had kissed her as if a goddess and she still tingled from the experience.

Carrie reflected on the inconsistency concerning societal rules and her classes: they were required to study lovers like Odysseus and Penelope, Aeneas and Dido, Antony and Cleopatra, and coerced into settling for second hand knowledge regarding passions of the heart. Considering the tragic, self-destructive results of these relationships, this attitude didn't make much sense to Carrie. How did she know whether these people were truly lovers or just dysfunctional? Their lack of discipline felled their own nations.

Carrie and her roommate met Ernie at the front of the dorm and drove together to the car rental agency. Another cross country runner by the name of Mike joined them there. Their assignment that day consisted of retrieving some stolen rental cars at the city pound. Ernie drove them to the city pound and inquired about the stolen cars. There were a few minor bureaucratic delays, but soon everyone in the group had a car to transport back to the agency.

Ernie led the procession while the rest of the drivers followed him through the industrial and business sections of town. Carrie soon learned that these drivers went through red lights and averaged eighty miles per hour in a forty miles per hour speed zone. These boys seemed protected by an invisible shield. Challenged to maintain a close distance behind Ernie, she found that he drove past her comfort zone. She could keep up with the boys or drop out. Not quite ready to drop out, Carrie sighed as she resolved to never get into a situation like this again. Never before had she broken so many rules in one afternoon, and perhaps served as the first time that she had broken any.

Finally reaching their destination, the drivers swerved into the agency parking lot and handed the keys over to the agency's mechanics.Then the group hopped in the back of Ernie's white truck for the return trip to the university. Reclining leisurely in the bed of the truck, Carrie watched the autumn sun sinking in the late afternoon glow and savored the grandeur of the day. The truck sped onto the main highway and she felt a gentle breeze tug at her hair, reminding Carrie of her evening plans with Marty. She looked forward to being with him again, instead of these ruffians. Experiences with Ellen, her younger sister, had taught her about the difference between spiritual rules and civil ones. She needed to get out of this situation before it became a perpetual, machismo rite of passage.

In the evening Marty took Carrie to a pub where they listened to a local rock band. While they sipped drinks and munched on nachos, they entertained each other with more stories about their interests and activities. The magic of the preceding encounter still remained. Without any conscious effort Marty and Carrie slipped into each other's lives as lovers. Afterwards, throughout the semester they met each other at dances, parties, between classes, and in the cafeteria without any formal arrangements. People immediately treated them as a couple and revealed where one could find the other without being asked.

Sometimes Marty and Carrie spent their evenings studying together, taking a break about midnight for a late evening stroll. One night, as they walked across the campus esplanade, Carrie nudged Marty's arm and whispered, "Let's climb that piece of modern art."

Several metal sculptures randomly dotted the campus for aesthetic purposes. Relaxing her shoulders with the peace of the outdoors, Carrie gazed at the hardy hunk of metal and relished the chance to stretch her upper body. She watched Marty amble up the huge black iron sculpture with the ease of his six foot three length. He smiled at her, obviously enjoying the climb, as well. He offered Carrie his hand and she joined him on the platform that stood about eight feet above the ground.

"Look at those stars!" Carrie exclaimed.

Marty beamed at her. The shadows of the sculpture camouflaged them from the wanderers on the mall below. They sat down on the platform and watched several figures walk across campus, completely unaware of their high perch.

"There goes Joe Romero probably on his way to see his girlfriend in Siena Hall," Marty whispered. Marty seemed to know everyone on campus and they all seemed to know him. "And here comes Frank and Tony..." he continued.

"Looks like the library just kicked everyone out," Carrie observed as she counted a few dozen students trickle out of the building. "That means that it must be one a.m.."

"This makes a good study break," Marty remarked with a yawn, drawing attention to their own little world on the sculpture's platform. After talking about their studies, classroom anecdotes, and other newsy tidbits, they eventually drifted to the subject of philosophy. "Ever read Bob Pitt's novel?" he asked.

"No, I haven't."

"I must give you the book sometime. It's about this guy who works on his car as if it is himself. He tours the country with his son while searching for meaning in life or what he calls the "Is"." Marty continued with a hint of sadness in his voice, "There's something I ought to tell you. Sometimes I have periods of time when I withdraw into a shell. I have a hard time believing in all the things that other people do like religion, humanity, peace, love...people, especially the religious ones, are such hypocrites. I just can't stand it. And love, what is love? How do people know when they are happy?" Marty recounted some of his frustrations with the members of his family and their ignorance of subjects such as philosophy. He claimed that most people were money-oriented and he cited his last girlfriend as an example.

Apparently she had dropped him for a wealthier fellow. Marty explained how different he seemed in comparison to other people he knew. He referred to himself as a cynic, because he felt unable to accept and enjoy the happier aspects of life. Everything seemed to be a facade; nothing seemed real or tangible. Carrie gripped the rim of the iron platform so that she wouldn't fall off. She watched Marty smile as he shook his head over his version of the world's affairs. He seemed to be enjoying his ideological isolation and his attempts to find the errors in his logic were feeble. Perhaps his former girlfriend had actually left him for a boyfriend with a richer perspective on life. Carrie loved Marty; regardless of her own differing feelings towards life, she didn't question his. She sensed that Marty didn't really believe his own convictions, being unaware of the extent which stubborn ideology influenced an individual's actions. In comparison, her attitude towards life favored optimism, and she couldn't agree with Marty and Nietzsche that god had died.

"I'm waiting for a revelation, a vision," he told her. "Then I'll change my mind. I'm open to new ideas and experiences that contradict my own. But, how does one really know without having a revelation confront them? It takes a revelation to change a person. Ever have a revelation?" he asked as he teasingly nudged Carrie's arm.

"Well, I have vision, my ideas...," she admitted cautiously, reluctant to buy into the revelations mandated by the good catholic boys serving as university professors.

"Like what?" Marty asked, still eager for a revelation.

"Nothing really earth shattering. Mostly just a series of isolated events wouldn't have much significance if I never bothered to string them together in a manner that provided meaning for me. It's hard to explain. I guess it just takes a lot of faith to believe in ideas and give them meaning. They become like a revelation for me, but I've never had one big experience that I could claim as a real revelation." Taking a deep breath, she recalled the good Catholic boys that raced the cars, and admitted, "Wake-up calls are not revelations; I prefer to see things coming before I get blind-sided."

"You'll have to tell me about these ideas sometime," Marty coaxed with a gentle grin. Hearing the chimes from the campus tower sounded the two o'clock notes, they began their descent from the sculpture's platform. "Looks like you're getting back to your dorm late again," Marty observed. Fortunately, the dorm had eliminated curfews years ago.

Chapter Eight

Experiences which lead to
Burning questions drive
Individuals to the depths

Tune Reference: *Carry On Wayward Son*

----Kansas

FOR THE ENTIRE semester Carrie experienced life without the Nightmare. When Marty left with the other half of his Sophomore class to study in Rome for half the year, the Nightmare returned. The new ideas raised in her classes and her relationship with Marty compelled Carrie to confront the Nightmare. Questioning the Nightmare's existence, she determined whether it existed solely in her imagination or as mental artifact. Armed with the logic gleaned in her classes, she transformed the Nightmare into a burden, rather than a death sentence. Finding it easier to carry the burden rather than deal with death, she concluded that this weight comprised the burden of proof.

However, Carrie found that she could relieve some of this weight in the letters she wrote to Marty. The letters served to formalized the concepts that freed her from the Nightmare. Though she had always trusted Marty's insight, the distance in their relationship increased her reliance on her own intuition. Unlike her english and philosophy papers, she worked to understand her own concepts before writing them down in a letter to Marty, who had already traversed the lies as an upperclassman. As a result of their ongoing dialogue, Marty and Carrie wrote each other many letters of great philosophical length throughout the semester.

For Christmas he had given her Bob Pitt's novel and she read the book over the holidays. The book proved excellent preparation for the metaphysics class that she took spring semester. All undergraduates were required to take Professor Fritz's class on Metaphysics. Many students referred to the instructor as MetaFist as they enjoyed watching the professor's absurd antics as he exhorted logic. He'd roar at the class and wave his cigar as if doing a Groucho Marx routine. "It's a paradox," he'd utter, chewing on a cigar which he later hurl at the class. The rash behavior contrasted with the supposed, higher ideals expressed in the course. Marty expressed anger at the hypocrisy, whereas Carrie became alarmed at the level of prestige that the professor entertained.

Eschewing the tests in literal regurgitation, Carrie and her friends memorized the concepts using the professor's same vocabulary. Meanwhile, rather than submit to this zombie state of affairs, Carrie developed her own concepts concerning metaphysics and exchanged her ideas with Marty. She desperately sought a satisfactory ideology which would allow her to come to deal with the Nightmare that haunted her. The professor, a reputable fascist, who had once smuggled for Spain, provided no explanation for the Nightmare's existence in the philosophies she studied in class. MetaFist's paradoxes failed to relate to the reality of the physical world, which made the Nightmare seemed even more elusive. Consequently, Carrie diverged from what she had been taught and came up with her own brand of Metaphysics to plot her course. She wrote Marty about her philosophy:

Dear Marty,

...finished reading Bob Pitt's book over the holidays. Seems that the car mechanic could have saved himself a lot of gas and energy if he had bothered to ground himself in human relationships before beginning his journey. I think the key to the story can be found at the end of the book when the mechanic realizes the importance of his relationship to his son. In the final episode, the ghost vanishes as the mechanic's relationship to his son materializes.

The story reminded me of a question that you asked me sometime ago during last semester, "what is truth?" I think that truth and love go hand in hand. MetaFist has been discussing the pursuit of truth in regards to Aquinas's concepts of Being and Essence, and he loves referring to "Paradoxical Structure of Existence." He seems to relish leaving the class hanging in paradoxes while he discusses aspects of being and nonbeing. Evidently, he can live with paradoxes in his life.

I don't particularly care for paradoxes myself, and view them as an indication that further questioning is needed for the sake of a resolution. Like life's little ironies, sometimes paradoxes reveal more about the nature of life than a straightforward answer, but they aren't an answer. I consider paradoxes to be similar to the koans offered by the zen masters where one actually must measure the reality of the situation in order to find it.

First I feel that truth does exist in today's world for those brave enough to merely apply a few basic principles. In discerning truth three properties must be examined: Esse, essence, and existence. Aquinas refers to Esse as the supreme essence of the object. I think of Esse as the single identity of an object in relation to its universal nature. Some zen artists might call it the "One." Essence refers to the nature of the object. Some might call it the "Many" because an object can have many different natures at once and still be the same object (Esse). The third property of existence describes the relationship of the object to the universe by virtue of its function and activity.

Seeking the truth forces the pursuer to employ these three properties. The next step involves the act of prescinding or cutting away valueless information concerning the subject. Care must be taken so that important information regarding the subject's nature (essence) is not overlooked. In other words, those who wish to delve in the heart of the matter must examine the subject in both its One and Many forms; truth is found in the correlation of a subject's existence to its Esse and essence.

Then, there is the question of finding truth in the form of concepts and ideas. The two properties examined in this instance are context and content. Content refers to the subject's matter. Context describes the relation of the matter to its universal whole. Once again both properties must be considered in terms of the One and Many. The prescinding operation must be utilized, waste discarded, and bammo! Truth emerges. I think MetaFist, Aristotle, Aquinas, and Pitts make it harder than it has to be. I see through the sexism of Rousseau, who they undermined by threading Hegel's distorted version of yin and yang. The Greeks and Romans Philosophers were gay and worshipped phallic symbols.

Within the next few weeks Marty sent Carrie the following reply:

Dear Carrie,

I agree with your idea that the book calls attention to the fact that one must find a ground in human relationships in order to comprehend meaning in life. Pitts takes a long time to reach this conclusion, and I feel that the book should have gone into this concept in more detail. It's so important.

Spent the spring break traveling alone through northern Europe. I'm going through one of my blue funks again. Wish you were here. The architecture of some of the churches and museums is really spectacular. The weather is very cold, but the people are warm and friendly. Stayed at a youth hostel in Sweden and learned of a castle in the area that serves as a learning center for Nietzsche's studies. I was impressed but I'm not sure if I can agree with all of Nietzsche's philosophies on life. The center seemed pretty open-minded though, and I had a good time rapping with the rest of the people there. I look forward to seeing you when I arrive in a few months.

Love,

Marty

Chapter Nine

Keep your shine

Despite the darkness

Tune Reference: *Sunshine*

----Jonathan Edwards

MARTY RETURNED FROM Rome a month after the spring semester ended. As Carrie met the passengers on the arriving flight from London, she easily distinguished Marty from the crowd by his long lean frame and bushy red beard which had grown during his travels. She ran to Marty immediately and wrapped him in her arms. Filtering from head to foot like a powerful light, an enormous smile flashed across the tall man's face.

"Hey, what's happening!" he greeted, apparently overwhelmed by Carrie's attention but enjoying it nonetheless.

"Good to see you!" Carrie answered before he swirled her around in the air with a mighty hug.

"Same here," he sighed as he put her down. "I've missed you. Like the beard?" he added. Then he made a funny face and tugged the hairs on his chin.

"Yes," she laughed. "Now you really look like a Viking."

Marty stayed a couple of days at Carrie's house before driving home to St. Louis. They had much news to tell each other and spent many hours discussing the events of the past semester. Marty emptied a pouch on the floor and went through his souvenirs.

"This is my favorite place," he told Carrie, handing her a postcard of Killarney, Ireland. "A friend and I camped one night in a pasture near Kerry. It's so peaceful in southern Ireland, not at like Belfast...And here, I brought this back for you." Marty pulled an Irish pound from his assortment of curios inside his traveling bag. "Ireland has very beautiful paper money," he commented while handing her the note.

"You're right," she commented. "This isn't money; this is art."

"Ya, I know. Look at the English pound," Marty replied as he pulled a wrinkled sample from his pocket. "Although the English receive more U.S. coins for their money, the Irish pound looks more valuable."

"The Irish pound is much prettier. I think I like it the best," Carrie said with a laugh. "Thank you very much."

"The artwork portrayed on the money has its own value," he observed. Then he began rummaging through the stack of travel booklets inside his case. After he found what he had been searching for, he handed Carrie a green pamphlet. "Oh, I also brought you a historical map of Ireland."

Carrie unfolded the map and laid it on the floor in front of her. Feeling the currency underneath her fingers as a direct link to the pulse of the country, she imagined what would be like to live in the foreign land. Meanwhile, Marty sustained her imaginary transition with a narration of his journeys there.

"My great grandmother came from southern Ireland," Carrie recalled after Marty had finished. "Sometimes my grandmother would tell me stories about her mother who immigrated to America. She told me how the Irish survived the potato famine. For dinner they placed a photo of a plate of food on the table before them. They stared at the picture and went through the motions of eating as if they were eating from a real plate. It required a great deal of concentration, but it prevented them from feeling the pains of hunger."

"How did their bodies handle the malnutrition?" Marty asked.

"She said that they still starved to death. They only fooled their bodies into blocking the pain."

"Mind over matter," Marty observed.

"Only to soothe the mind itself."

****

"To soothe the mind itself," Carrie murmured under her breath as she stood squarely on the end of the diving board high above the swimming pool. Alone in her world on top of the diving platform, Carrie broke from her silent thoughts to survey the scene below her. Like the others waiting patiently behind her, the party held no interest for her. A few people at the pool party stopped and watched the parade of divers in the crisp night air. The rest were deeply absorbed in their conversations and paid little attention to the small group of divers perfecting their flights over the blue waters.

"One swan dive in perfect grace and form," she told herself before she began the motion.

Bbberrummph! The diving board echoed as Carrie sprang off its edge and flew into the beauty of a starry night. With her arms held wide in the air to embrace all the warmth the dark air could offer, she strained every muscle against the earth's gravity. Once she achieved maximum height she let the earth catch her. Then she arched her body until the head was lower than her feet, maintaining straightness and poise throughout the motion.

Carrie entered the water like a knife slicing through the waves with the lightest of splashes. Deep below the surface, she flipped her feet around her and pushed off from the pool's bottom. Within a few seconds Carrie appeared on top of the surface like a cork bobbing in tub of water and swam to the water's edge.

One swan dive with grave difficulty, she quietly told herself as she heaved her sopping wet body over the pool's tiled wall. Her thoughts came from the memory of high school diving meets where the judges always prefaced scores with such terminology. Tonight in her solo competition Carrie played all the roles: judge, spectator, coach, and diver.

As she waited her turn on the high board her thoughts returned to the other concerns in her life at the moment.

"I'm not sure I can say, 'I love you' anymore," Marty had told her inside the empty restaurant during a midsummer's evening. Though his words stunned Carrie, she decided not to press the issue. At the time Carrie had wanted to give him freedom to air his emotions regardless of the pain she felt. Realizing that Carrie wasn't going to question his feelings, Marty immediately relaxed and sought her hand.

Placing her hands on the cold steel ladder leading to the diving board, Carrie began the ascent for another dive. Marty lived a few hours away from the university now. Over the last summer, he decided to major in computer science and transferred to a state university. With this new sense of direction Marty appeared much happier with himself. He enjoyed his course of study and no longer brooded over heavy philosophical diversions. In spite of the positive changes in his life, Marty continued to bury himself in his habitual shell, pushing Carrie away from him in the process.

Reaching the top of the metal diving platform, Carrie stood upright and waited for the previous diver to exit the area directly below the board.

She felt a cool breeze brush across the pool's surface. She wanted to catch a ride with the moving wind as soon as possible. Quickly Carrie sprang off the diving hurling past the water's hard surface.

Deep in the blue depths more thoughts about Marty entered her head. Often during their discussions, Carrie assumed the positive and fought the negative while Marty accepted the negative and questioned the positive. The issues Marty raised were echoes in her own mind, They both knew that their debates with each other were also debates with themselves. Carrie played the part of the optimist whereas Marty chose to be the cynic. They played their roles very well, each trying to convince the other of their own argument; and most of the time the debates ended with the two laughing at their predictable responses.

The night with Marty in the restaurant had been different. There had been no prescribed roles or responses; they had been dealing with reality instead. It marked a turning point in their former light-hearted relationship, which suddenly reflected the problems Marty had with his father. Though, his father had abandoned his family several years ago, Marty had not got over it like the other members. Instead, he pursued the relationship, like a haunted character in a Bob Pitt novel.

Another dive. Carrie didn't want to be dragged down by her emotional dramas anymore; she wanted to rise above the surface of this present existence. Stretching high above the pool's surface, she rose above the scene below her. Then she plummeted to the depths, breaking the surface's impact with her fists to save herself from the effects on her skull.

"I can't say, 'I love you,'" Marty told her in the restaurant that night. He had pulled his negative trump card, and Carrie acquiesced. Marty had contaminated their relationship with his feeling on his parents divorce.

Carrie recalled his words as she pulled out of her underwater descent. Then she focused on Marty. She could not change him. Her parents had also divorced, but she remained optimistic that there were people who could say "I love you" without denying it or turning it into a philosophical debate. Other people took the plunge. After climbing to the height of the board, Carrie paused briefly before starting her next dive. *Had Brian felt this way before jumping off the stadium?* He had served as an altar boy for the priest, who presided over the memorial service. The priest's cold manner seemed to offhandedly condemn the young man, for reasons unavailable to the public.

I just want to fly too, Carrie told herself. She remained safe as long as she focused on her actions. *I have con-tro-o-ol*, Carrie mentally reminded herself as she tensed certain muscles for the timing of the dive. Discipline had become the first topic of her conversation with Marty.

Attaining total muscle control on this dive, she later felt the waves rush over her rapidly submerging form. For her next dive Carrie imagined being Brian. *All I know is that I love you*, she expressed to the world during her silent flight, as she sensed the impact of such a love. Conscious of its effect, she struck the water below. Carrie watched the waves crash around her head and rip past her body. After rising to the surface, she concluded that Brian must have been in a daze to attempt a dive from such heights.

Carrie hurried to the top of the ladder again. Brian had died, while Carrie still lived with the Nightmare. Like any dive, forays into the subconscious could be fatal if she didn't focus on her activities. Standing perfectly still at the far end of the board, she steadied her form and concentrated on the dive before beginning her next attempt. *Yes, you can fly whenever you wish*, she reminded herself. *Just keep your motions free and safe. Protect yourself from injury in your form.* Executing this intention high over the pool, Carrie assumed the grace of a spirited swan. She completed the dive in a matter of seconds, fast and unrestrained. She exited the pool and stepped onto the concrete edge. She had mastered her dives, control;ing their momentum almost like automation. As a result, theory had become reality. Soon she might even be able to face the emotional force of the Nightmare without being threatened. *Brrerumph!* the diving board resonated as another diver flew over the pool. Carrie turned and watched his effortless motions. She curiously wondered what other divers thought about during their jumps.

Chapter Ten

Wolves may come to destroy shelters

Created by the piggish

The best defense is to either

Be with the wind

Or withstand the wind

Which may require wit

Tune Reference: *Wild World*

----Cat Stevens

AS CARRIE MASTERED her emotions and physical body in the blue heights above the swimming pool, her assignments in physics encouraged her to define her perceptions of the physical world through controlled experiments. The Nightmare complicated her life. Like most physicists, she craved simple explanations. The notion of reducing all the affairs in her life to mathematical equations inspired Carrie to take a different approach. Unlike metaphysics, physics brought the intangible world within her grasp so that she could understand it in simple terms. Physics sought an inherent understanding of the universe. The discipline pursued the root causes of phenomenon. When it came to questioning the universe, Carrie found that the physicists had the most fun; they applied principles they learned in class to the experiences of their own lives, breathing life into their academic lessons.

The Physics department at the university consisted of two instructors. Professor Max, a gracefully aged Romanian, served as chairman. The youthful assistant professor, called Dr. C. by his students, bemoaned the fact that many of his students could not pass his tests. The teaching style of the two men differed immensely, but those who were fortunate to study under both discovered that the different approaches complemented each other.

Carrie studied under Professor Max for her second semester physics class with eight other students. After growing accustomed to the thick Slavic accent, she only had to follow the professor's metaphysical diversions. "Phee-zeeks," Professor Max told them, served as the most truthful of the sciences, following behind philosophy and mathematics in the hierarchy of disciplines which studied the dynamics of the universe.

More than any other scientist Carrie had ever known, Dr. C. enjoyed toying with the rules in the physical universe. The young, silver-haired physicist from an ivy league school often to climb the science building to retrieve the various gadgets set in flight during his lecture. His lectures were the results of his raids on toy departments at local dime stores. He possessed a mechanical bird that could fly powered by a wound-up rubber band and conservation of energy. He tossed frisbees to demonstrate principles of angular momentum and inertia. Once he even held class at the local honky tonk to discuss the special physics of beer bubbles. More concerned with the pragmatic side of physics, Dr. C.'s toys demonstrated the importance of physical knowledge in the world.

Having realized the value of adult play in the world, Carrie marveled at the tales told about the manner Dr. C. played this knowledge to his advantage. She noticed how Dr. C. inspired his students to seemingly bend the rules of the physical universe during the process, which played on the theory of relativity. Without any personal interaction with the instructor, she discovered the usefulness of such fantastical pursuits, especially for individuals with limited resources. For this topic in physics, Dr. C.'s most instructive hour usually came during the week when students raised money for charity. Traditionally, academicians devoted one day of charity week exclusively to the disruption of classes. Both students and professors could have their instructors or classes thrown into jail for a fee determined by the size of the class. These circumstances often pitted students and faculty into direct financial confrontation. Some students skipped class, some professors cancelled class, and others eagerly paid the price to send the other party to jail. Stalemates were broken by the highest bidder and often nobody knew who had won until the jailers hauled them away.

Dr. C. always tried to cut expenses with his attempts to outsmart the jailers (who were usually members of the Knights of Oblivion, the sanctioned occult group haunting campus grounds) with physics. Most of Carrie's friends applauded anyone besting the K of O at their violent games, in the nightmarish land of the reactivated KKK and graveyard hangings. His first experiment made its debut two years ago, when he showed how a handful of rope and a small four ounce pulley could support a chair and one Physics professor clutching a physics book. The advanced physics majors tested the apparatus with a nonmajor before suspending the instructor to a height of twenty-five feet. When the jailers arrived to seize the professor, they found him conducting class from his swing over the lecture hall. After making many futile attempts to coax Dr. C. down from his perch, the jailers resorted to spraying him down with a garden hose from the campus grounds. Then they carried the drenched professor to jail.

The next year Dr. C. resorted to electrical power as a defense. Armed with an electric cattle prod, he encamped himself behind a network of barb wire standing in the lecture room. His position placed him beside the electrical wall outlet and enabled him to prod the jailers as they entered the room. The only recourse for the frustrated jailers was to pull the circuit for the entire building. Without the least hesitation or consideration for other ongoing classes in the building, they turned off the power source and hauled the professor away in the dark.

By Carrie's sophomore year, Dr. C.'s class act became even more elaborate. He rented a white limo to drop him off at the front of the lecture building, and emerged from the car attired in a white suit with matching white cowboy hat and boots. From the crowd of students curiously gathered around the limo, there appeared six physics majors dressed in black suits and masked in dark sunglasses who stood next to Dr. C. and escorted him to class.

In class Dr. C. explained the Faraday principle and later proved that a electrical charge could indeed reside on the surface of a closed conductor. Underneath his white suit Dr. C. had clothed his body in a shield of aluminum foil. This suit of aluminum foil served as Dr. C.'s closed conductor. After breaker, he plugged the Van der Graaf generator into the guarded wall socket and placed one hand on its silver globe.

After spending twenty minutes overcoming the physics majors guarding the circuit breaker, the jailers that reached Dr. C. received a blue spark that arced at least a foot. The professor also hurled a few streaks of lightning at nearby metallic objects for dramatic effect. Again the jailers pulled the circuit breaker for the entire building and Dr. C. lost his charge source. The jailers, ignorant in the basic principles of physics, lunged for the professor when they realized that the generator had been turned off. Since a charge will continue to reside on the surface of a closed conductor until that conductor is properly grounded, the first few jailers touching the professor were shocked with a dazzling blue arc. Consequently, they served as the human ground for discharging the electrical energy from the professor's metallic suit. Without suffering any personal discomfort during the entire episode, Dr. C. had enough juice to zap four jailers after losing his power source. It took a moment for the puzzled jailers to recover from their bewilderment and resume their efforts in capturing the professor. Eventually, they succeeded and led Dr. C. away to the cardboard prison in the student activity center. There he joined a few students and faculty members who were just striking up a poker game, while a philosophy professor practiced on his violin in another corner of the enclosure.

Under the silent fatherly eye of the department chairman, the student physicists continued to mimic Dr. C.'s fun throughout the year and create an active learning environment for participants. The only other female physics major lived just down the hall from Carrie's dorm room. Phyllis was a junior level physics major. For her birthday someone decorated her room in lengthy swirls of toilet paper. The culprit left a message inscribed in red lipstick on her mirror: Happy Birthday, Phyllis! XX Dr. C.. Dr. C. vehemently denied any involvement with the room papering when confronted with the evidence. People believed that Dr. C had been framed and the identity of the joker remained a mystery.

As a result of these paper capers, it surprised no one except Dr. C. when he unlocked his office door one morning and walked into a forest of multicolored bathroom tissue. Dr. C. remained speechless, flashing a large poster with the message HELP to whomever happened to be walking down the hall. Even the brilliant professor admitted that whoever had been responsible for the caper was a master artist; he could not conceive of the mode of entry into the office, except through the locked door.

Only Professor Max proved exempt from these feats in the Physics department, though the adjoining city of Dallas became an unwitting participant. Students who spent late evening hours in the laser lab would sometimes take the helium-neon laser outside for a midnight stroll. They discovered that many spectacular effects could be produced by bouncing the monochromatic light beam at the clouds hovering over a nearby football stadium. The laser light crisscrossing the area. Some of the cars even stopped and pulled over to the side of the road. Although the class never read about the results of their experiment in the newspapers the next day, they couldn't help wonder whether people on the highway could distinguish a laser light show from an unidentified flying object. Yet, when it came to demonstrating the wizardry of physics, Professor Max reigned. As most therapists claimed psychology to be the basis of the occult, Professor Max used psychological motivations to extract magical phenomenon. The older professor taught Carrie the importance of being able to approach life's challenges from the perspective of a physicist. At the beginning of every year, Professor Max shook the dust from boxes containing the most famous experiments in the history of physics. Then he handed the boxes to his students with the instructions to repeat the observations. Everyone in class, were simply a matter of faith and obstinacy on the part of the experimenters.

Carrie never could decide what motivated Millikan to painstakingly spray a charge on a tiny oil drop, suspend it in an electric field until the oil drop remained motionless, and then measure the charge of an electron by determining the electric force needed to hold the drop stationary. Millikan became the first to record the charge to mass ratio of an electron. What caused him to make the leap of faith and initially consider the possibility? What led him to believe that his experimental approach to the problem would ever succeed? What kept him going through all those years of trying to balance an oil drop in an electric field? She experienced only a portion of the frustration in the university laboratory; and she already knew the results.

Of course, Carrie wondered whether the forebears of physics actually created their own reality through the design of their experiments. Could a scientist affect the outcome of the experiment with his expectations of what the results should be? Conceivably, anyone could cause an experiment swearing an oath or pretending to be an impartial observer? Could mere faith find the truth in spite of human limitations?

The Michelson-Morley experiment upheld the notion that truth exists on its own merit. They proved that imagination could not affect the final outcome of an experiment, because the results of their experiment were beyond anyone's wildest predictions. Scientists once believed that electromagnetic waves such as light were propagated in a medium called the ether. Light moved through the ether in the same manner that a person swims in a stream; the time required to cross the stream depended on whether the individual swam with the current or against it. The ether wind or current resulted from the revolution of the earth around the sun, analogous to the wind a person feels when hanging an arm outside the window of a moving car. Michelson and Morley wished to detect this ether current by measuring the velocity of light moving parallel and perpendicular to this stream. The differing velocities in these two courses of travel would be due to the motion of the ether. Surprisingly, Michelson and Morley failed to detect a change in the speed of light as it moved through the ether. There was no ether wind to disrupt the flow of light. It didn't matter whether the ether actually existed because the speed of light remained absolute; one could only acknowledge what affected one's universe. Many people repeated this same experiment because they personally disagreed with the implications. Many added their own variations. Some tried it at different parts of the world. Some performed the experiment at different times of the year. Others propagated the light travel at different angles with respect to the ether stream. Everyone obtained the same results: the earth moved at rest relative to the ether like a motionless car without gas.

These astounding results forced reevaluation of Newton's mechanical universe, something that the French had promoted for years. The acceptance of this experiment did not guarantee the understanding the phenomena. Twenty years elapsed before a satisfactory explanation was found in Einstein's special theory of relativity. No longer could the universe be viewed from a mechanical perspective; it had many dimensions and apparently some absolutes.

Armed with a historical perspective, Carrie learned to believe in the unseen universe, especially since she preferred staying out of the wizardry fray and never witnessed any of these academic schemes. Instead, she savored the usefulness of her imagination in devising experiments and equipment that placed it within her view. With this ability to separate imagination from intuitive reality, she developed a sixth sense for the feel of her world through scientific methods. Carrie transformed all of her senses, intuitions, fantasies into experiences that could be analyzed by her intellect. She learned how to make the impossible seem valid by just conjuring the possibilities; thereby, learning how to decide what really could not be. This kept her out of the realm of occultism, while bringing magic back into her life, like a shiny blue baton beating back a closet of displaced emotions.

Chapter Eleven

Believe or not

Some people

Emphasize with the devil

Tune Reference: *Sympathy For The Devil*

----Rolling Stones

CARRIE LEARNED HOW to accept the Nightmare's reality without bothering to prove the Nightmare's existence. After Professor Max and Dr. C. made it all seem so easy, she began to believe in the power of her own abilities. Yet, in spite of the strides Carrie made in dealing with the various intangible realities in her life, some events occurred which brought her dangerously close to the Nightmare's death grip. Though Carrie could greatly control the physical environment of the swimming pool and laboratory, there were other events in her life which she could not alter. As consequence, she did not foresee what would happen on the night of freshman initiation or do much to avoid the circumstances. This single event catalyzed a turn in her life, despite the ongoing nightmarish conditions in the environment.

One early autumn weekend, Marty and Carrie spent the afternoon at a state park located two miles north of campus. Many towering oaks filled the park making it an ideal birding habitat. Jays and robins hopped in the brush as raptors circled above them. The couple hiked several miles inside the park before deciding to stop for a picnic.

"The park ranger knows every bird call from the golden eagle to the Concorde jet," Carrie told Marty. "We met him when our biology class hiked through here last spring."

"Looks like things are getting run down," Marty remarked as he noticed the beer bottles lying in the brush nearby.

"Yeah, it was much cleaner for the spring class. I wonder what happened over the summer," Carrie replied as they approached the trail sign at the end of their hike. After a moment's reflection, she stooped down to pick up some litter and explained, "They started holding rallies last August. Returning home from work one night, my sister took a detour down some dirt roads in the valley. There were a bunch of men in white sheets burning crosses..."

"Are you kidding?" Marty asked.

"My sister got out of there really quick." Then she continued, "Someone in the dorm mentioned last year that they were burning crosses on people's lawns in her hometown." Carrie looked at the eagle soaring in the sky overhead. Then she peered at Marty. "When I was in high school, we had incidences of hangings and dead cats in local cemeteries. The town newspapers traced it to some sort of devil cult that had fascinated a few teenagers in a wealthy neighborhood." Carrie walked on, "I know the cemetery. Its just a little pioneer graveyard like all the others scattered around the Chisholm trail that went through my backyard."

Carrie and Marty reached the trailhead at the park's entrance and put down their packs for a break. They examined the sign for a map, however some odd scripted letters and symbols caught Carrie's eye on the back of the wooden sign. "Oh no!" she exclaimed as she took a step back. "It looks like the occultists have been here too!"

Marty fearfully eyed the writing on the back of the sign. He and Carrie hurriedly grabbed their packs and began hiking towards the road. "That park ranger won't be happy to see those engravings on the back of his park sign. I wonder if he has seen it yet," Carrie commented, breaking the silence once they were a quarter of a mile down the road. "Another person in the dorm told a bunch of us in the dorm last week about stumbling across an occult gathering in one of the men's dorms. She and two men were looking for a quiet place to study. Nobody knew about it. She warned us not to go to any study groups there. She wouldn't go into details...she seemed pretty shocked by what she saw."

"Which dorm was it?" Marty quizzed her.

"Ignatius," she told him. "The biology teaching assistant said that the local priest was pursuing some black rose cult on campus."

When they reached campus, they went straight to Marty's car in the parking lot. Having transferred to another college, Marty placed his pack in the car and prepared for his drive. Sitting behind the wheel, he inventoried the contents of the car, and sat behind the wheel. Then he rolled down his window and sought Carrie's kiss.

"I'll see you in two weeks," he said, gripping the wheel firmly. "Are you going to see the Senior's skits tonight?"

At the beginning of every year, some upperclassmen in the women's dorm would perform a series of skits on how to survive life at the university. Although they called their show "Freshman Initiation," it offered friendly advice without any hazing. Many representatives from all classes, men and women, came to enjoy the hilarious satires.

"Yes, I'm going to meet some people from my dorm and walk over at eight tonight."

"Have fun," Marty wistfully said with a wave. Then he backed his car out of the lot and sped off.

Later that evening, Carrie and her friends walked to the lobby of the of the women's dorm. They found it filled to capacity. Carrie personally knew several of the seniors, having attended the same grade school. She marveled at their sophisticated interpretations of campus affairs, as they had always impressed her with their talented sketches. Shortly before the performance of the last skit, a low rumble rose from outside the dorm.

"It's the K of O," someone whispered. K of O referred to Knights of Oblivion, an illicit fraternity which met every Thursday night to lose sobriety. The meetings were held in the woods surrounding the campus at a location marked by an enormous bonfire. Usually by sophomore year, most men on campus had attended at least one K of O meeting. Many men sought to assert their masculinity through alcohol consumption.

Occasionally some of Carrie's male friends attended the meetings to obtain a free beer, but they never bothered to linger. They claimed that the K of O became rowdier in direct proportion to the amount of alcohol consumed. Women were not allowed at the meetings and the women on campus would have preferred seeing the group disbanded because of their violent fits, which promoted an inane type of machismo on campus. The K of O had their own brutal version of freshman initiation, though their commitment varied from year to year. Some years they never even bothered with the rite. Their rite consisted of intoxicating all the men on campus, freshmen in particular, beating them up and then marching on the women's freshman dorm. Adhering to the late medieval style of the Goths and Vandals, the K of O would hose down the surrounding terrain with water and create a giant moat around the dorm. Then they would pelt the building with rocks and mud balls. Men from their ranks would be assaulted as well. Once they broke into the dorm, they would drag its inhabitants outside and stone them. School leaders served as prime targets.

This year the K of O seemed more rabid than previous years for the resident assistants were drug from the dorm within only fifteen minutes. The loss of the resident assistants rendered the dorm defenseless, creating confusion and panic among the terrified freshmen. Without vehicles to leave campus, freshmen hid in their rooms and locked their doors, The Knights of Oblivion burst through the doors in the main entrance and grabbed anybody standing near the entrance. Kicking and screaming, the victims were carried outside and thrown in the mud. With no one left in charge of the dorm, the inhabitants panicked.

"Lock up the side entrance!" Someone shouted. "We can't let them get in!" Meanwhile, other people rushed to protect the front entrance. By the second attack all of the seniors and resident assistants had been captured. The remaining juniors and sophomores assumed responsibility for the welfare of the people inside.

A volley of rocks and wooden poles shook the building. Instantly, all the lights went out as the K of O cut off the electric power. A series of screams pierced the darkness and continued to echo throughout the two floors of the dormitory. Through the dark shadows Carrie followed her older friends down the hallway and to the building's side entrance. They joined the efforts of several others who were pushing the door closed, while Carrie gathered some metal poles to brace the door shut and relieve the group's hold. More heavy objects struck the walls of the side entrance.

"Oh no! They're gonna break the windows!" Someone whispered. Tall plate glass windows towered above the heads of those defending the entry hall. If any window shattered, the entire group would be one bloody mess.

"I heard that they were not going to come this year," Carrie mentioned to a student council representative who was helping her gather the poles. Her words could hardly be heard above the din.

"Me too," she said. "A man at the bonfire said that some of the guys really got drunk and became mean. He watched it all. He left early to warn the dorm. Somebody should call campus police...Help!" she hollered while hurrying to the door that was about to be attacked for a second time. "Call security!" she authorized.

Just as she left the vicinity, the door was suddenly jerked from the hands of those trying to keep it closed. Twenty to thirty men dressed in the medieval garb of the K of O rushed at the small group in entry hall. They seized Carrie and tossed her in the air, before hurling her in a pit of rocks and mud. Thrashing wildly, Carrie fought those trying to hold her down. Out of the corner of her eye she noticed two other members of the K of O come towards her with their arms full of mud, gravel, and cut glass. Then she turned her face away from the onslaught of stones and dirt. Closed her eyes, Carrie spun her body like a hurricane against her attackers. Surrounding herself in a tight swirling vortex of light, she swung her wildly at those attempting to hurt her. They became immediately discouraged and left. After her attackers went away Carrie remained motionless in the mud for several long seconds. She wondered how many people had been assaulted that night. She imagined that the initiation for freshman boys had been worse, because the Knights of Oblivion seized more liberties with their own gender. The symbolism of the mud and the sexual tone of the assault jarred her. One month they roughed people up in the name of charity and in the next month they attacked those new to the campus.

Carrie quickly leaped to her feet as she surveyed her surroundings. What had began as a fun relaxed gathering for coeds had turned into a ghastly event. People hurled weapons all around her, but none of it seemed aimed for her, just another grime-covered body in the throng and relatively safe now. Carrie searched the crowd for signs of the group who had been drug from the side entry. She wondered what had happened to them. Instead of leaving, she launched a counter-attack. Picking up a handful of mud, she threw it at a man preparing to pole open the entrance to the dorm. The man dropped the pole when the wad hit him on the side of the face. He froze as he realized that a woman had just clobbered him with his own mess. A group of women from the dorm windows cheered Carrie. Carrie ducked and gathered another mud ball. She threw another in the man's direction and missed. Despite the missed shot, the women in the dorm screamed with delight and muted the frenzied howls below. The man turned towards Carrie and sighed. The happy yells supporting Carrie's attack had taken the steam out his. Some men who had been assaulted fought for the pole. Another grime-covered woman appeared to Carrie's right and slapped a hand of mud on the head of a nearby Knight of Oblivion. The women from the window quickly became inspired and started dropping buckets of water on the heads of attackers.

The mob went away. Some Knights of Oblivion doggedly continued as if in a trance. Carrie watched the hate and sadness in the eyes of the attackers grow and grow, emptying their spirit like a cancer. Dorm defenders exuberantly danced around them and toppled the deflated attacker into the mud. The defeated men didn't get replaced.

Carrie turned and walked up the ridge behind her. As she started to climb the slope she spotted a friend of Marty's from the cross-country team. Still wearing his running shorts from practice, he slowly sipped a beer while maintaining a watchful eye on the chaos below.

"Hi," she said, throwing some mud on the ground near his feet. She purposely missed him.

"Hi," he replied, returning the mud toss without malice. The volley missed Carrie by several feet. A few seconds of silence elapsed before she joined him at the top.

"It's pretty wild down there," he said grimly.

Carrie turned around to survey the activity after she found a safe distance from the scene below. She had broken the pattern by leading the counter attack. Future K of O assaults would be opposed. She noted the difference between this university and other schools. Students at other colleges experimented in love-making; this one regressed to barbaric medieval tortures, which scarred the campus terrain.

"Ya, I'm going back to my dorm," she decided in a hushed voice. Still shaking from the trauma of the experience, her legs weakly supported her stance.

Without saying another word, he escorted Carrie over to the other side of campus. He left her alone at the water faucet where she hosed the blood and dirt off her body before entering the dorm. Although Carrie still felt emotionally drained, physical damage amounted to a few cuts and bruises. The water felt warm to her touch and it restored strength to her aching limbs. After rinsing her body, Carrie turned off the water and sat down on a nearby concrete step.

She looked up from the earth's darkness for the soft white glow of the moon, located in the middle of the star studded sky. Carrie sighed as she began to feel safe in her world again. The magic of the moonlight shone through the night and soothed her wounds and emotions. Then she rose and limped up the stairs leading to her room in the dorm.

"What happened to you?" her roommate asked Carrie.

"Freshman initiation...K of O attacked the dorm and we beat the hell out of them," she responded as headed straight for a hot shower.

The next morning she attended classes as usual and saw her friends from the dorm in the cafeteria during lunch. Following their cue, nobody mentioned the event of the previous evening, except noting the muddy footprints found in the dorm's hall this morning. Connie revealed that security had arrived shortly after she left. Although, the Knights of Oblivion continued to be an institution on campus, their activities faded into obscurity.

Chapter Twelve

It doesn't take tequila

To see a brilliant sunrise

Or pursue a dream

Tune Reference: *Tequila Sunrise*

----Eagles

AN AFRICAN AMERICAN from Carrie's third year calculus class captained her intramural volleyball team. Named Darlene, she sat at the back of the class with several other outspoken individuals, and kept tabs on the instructor's calculations. When they weren't busy watching the professor, they played amongst themselves. Despite the distractions caused by this group, the professor thrived on their attention. The mild heckling remained jovial and rescued the class from a dry lecture.

One of Darlene's friends, a tall, skinny fellow with a scraggly beard, endlessly toted a camera around his neck. He usually came to class wearing a Greek sailor's cap, black leather jacket, and dark glasses. He reminded Carrie of an ex-motorcycle rider who had been dropped by his gang for wearing a cheesy smile. When he wasn't busy taking pictures for the yearbook and school newspaper, he played volleyball with a team called the "Swans" or followed Darlene around. Darlene also coached the "Swans," a motley group of sophomore men who named the team after a fairy tale about a young princess with six brothers.

Escape from Oblivion

Carrie had always been fascinated by the fairy tale of the princess and six swans. According to the story, an evil witch transformed the six princes into swans. In order to free her brothers from the enchantment, the young princess sewed six shirts out of star flowers within six years. She could not speak or laugh during this period. In spite of her silence, she managed to marry a king and birth three children. However, the evil queen stole the children and claimed that the princess had killed them. Just as the princess faced execution for the crime, she threw the shirts on her brother swans and transformed them into princes again. The princess proclaimed her innocence, the evil queen died in a freak accident, and the children were returned to their parents. Although the fairy tale ended happily, there remained one minor problem; the princess had been unable to finish the sleeve of the sixth shirt and the youngest brother retained a swan wing.

In contrast to the horrific tensions resulting from the dorm attacks, the men's adaptation of the fairy tale moved Carrie. She also juxtaposed fantasy with reality for amusement; sometimes Carrie identified with the mute princess and other times she related to the prince with the remaining swan wing. Whenever she practiced her high dives, Carrie tried to be as graceful as a swan. She admired the princess' determination to knit a happy endings into the given situation.

Obviously, the Swan with the cheesy smile cultivated an infatuation with Darlene, his volleyball coach. He trailed her almost everywhere, usually about two steps behind. Darlene enjoyed his company but never supported his romantic interest. During a campus blood drive, Carrie became better acquainted with Darlene's Swan. Though Carrie had donated blood before without any adverse effects, she became more anxious than usual while lying on the table waiting for the extraction of the usual pint. Her blood pumped slowly and she became lightheaded. Taking her mind off her predicament,

Carrie initiated conversation with the guy lying head to head with her on the next table. Neither could see each other. "Ever done this before?" she asked him.

"No."

"What class are you in?"

"Sophomore. What class are you in?"

"Sophomore."

"Going to Rome?"

"Yah, I plan to go early and travel through England and Ireland. I've always wanted to visit those countries. Do you know Claire and Jan?"

"Yes," he said with excitement in his voice.

"We plan to fly together to London. A lot of people are meeting in London. Mike is throwing a party on January 10th. Any university traveler in England is invited. After the party Claire, Jan, and I plan to buy a BritRail pass and go to Ireland. Then we'll ride the Eurail to the Rome campus...By the way my name is Carrie Jackson."

"Brent Wright. I haven't really made any plans for my travels yet."

"You're welcome to see my maps on the countries. I can give you directions to Mike's place and we can arrange to meet in London. If you are interested in going through Ireland, you could even travel with us to Rome."

"I like your plans. Could I look over your maps this afternoon?"

"I'm free at one o'clock but I leave for work at three. I'm a lifeguard for the campus swimming pool," she told him. "My room number is 324 in Patrick Hall. Just give my room a buzz and I'll meet you in the lobby. Where are you from originally?"

"Vermont. My parents own ten acre farm near the mountains. We have a few cows and chickens, and grow our own fruits and vegetables."

"What brings you to Texas?"

"I have a scholarship. I plan to get a master's degree in applied solar engineering after I complete my physics degree. I'll graduate in three years instead of the usual four years. Because I'm interested in engineering, Professor Max is allowing me to substitute some engineering courses from a state university for some of my physics work. After I return to the United States, I plan to spend the summer in the area. I already have several jobs at the university waiting for me, in addition to the two or three courses I'll be taking this summer."

"I'm interested in studying solar energy too. In high school I built a solar-powered radio for a science fair project. By using an earphone I minimized the amount of power drawn by the amplifier...It actually worked! I heard music from some of the bigger stations...Last summer I made a solar oven."

"How hot did you get your solar oven?"

"400 degrees Fahrenheit on a typical summer's day of 100 degrees Fahrenheit. I never tried to bake anything in it, though. I ran out of time."

"My father and I built a solar greenhouse last summer. We added some ventilation to the original design because the greenhouse became too hot. I did it just like a real engineer," Brent said in a voice suggesting that he remained awestruck by the accomplishment. "I drew the blueprints and had a city inspector approve my design before ever beginning the project. We used fiberglass for the sides and made an insulated base from styrofoam. Originally, we planned to heat the house by opening the structure to my parent's bedroom window. But Mom doesn't like the earthy smell of a greenhouse, so we closed the opening. Now my Dad grows his tomatoes and starts seedlings for his garden inside the greenhouse."

"That sounds neat!" Carrie exclaimed, impressed by this unidentified talker. Then she added, "I'm a physics major also. I'm about a course behind because I changed my major from chemistry. I'm making up for lost time with summer school. Do you have Dr. C. for any of your classes?"

"I'm taking his electromagnetics course. We papered his office about two weeks ago."

"So you're the one who pulled it off!" She smiled with the realization that her blood donation had become a serendipity.

Without being asked, Brent exuberantly volunteered the intricacies of the prank. "I popped the ceiling panels above the electronics lab and crawled over to his office. The lab is next to his room and I all I had to do was remove the ceiling panel from Dr. C.'s office. I landed on his desk. It helps to be tall and skinny. Then I unlocked the door and helped Betty paper the room. She supplied the paper; she wanted to get even with Dr. C. for papering her dorm room."

"But Dr. C. insists that he wasn't responsible for that one."

"I know...I did it," he confessed. I opened a window from the room next door and walked across the outside ledge. Betsy left one of her windows open, so I crawled through it and papered her room. Then I left a message in regardless of the message."

"So who did our room?"

"The younger brother of your dorm mate across the hall. He always uses computer paper. For my birthday they filled my room with millions of tiny paper dots from the computer sheets. I found paper dots in my drawers, my socks, my shoes, my books, my camping gear...I'm still finding dots in my things."

"Looks like you're finished," a blood technician announced as she walked over to Brent. After releasing him, she glanced at the measly amount in Carrie's bag, she observed, "You seem to be going rather slowly...keep pumping that blood." Then she left.

Finally able to solve the mysterious identity of the adjacent conversationalist, Brent hopped to his feet and walked towards Carrie. She nodded, recognizing him as Darlene's Swan.

"See ya at one o'clock. Take it easy, lady." Then he left to relax at the recovery station.

She watched the bag of blood hanging over her right arm. Not even half full, she focused on pumping her blood faster so that she could get out of the place. The procedure took much longer than anticipated and everyone else seemed to donate at a faster rate.

After forever passed, a technician finally came and pulled the needle from Carrie's arm. "You're done," she said. "How are you feeling?"

"OK," Carrie responded, anxiously glancing at the clock. She had been on the table for over thirty minutes. Though she possessed low blood pressure like most athletes, Carrie really felt that she spent too much for the donation.

She slowly rose from the table and walked towards the recovery station, but never made it that far. Within the same minute she collapsed on the floor and awoke staring at the white collar of a priest. Much to Carrie's relief, he never asked her whether she wanted the Last Rites. Shocked by the presence of the seminarian hovering overhead and her prone position on the ground, she left the premises as soon as her legs supported her.

Late in the afternoon Brent came by her dorm to see Carrie's maps of Ireland and England. "You have quite a collection here," he commented afterwards. Impressed by the thoroughness of her travel plans, he decided, "I'll meet you in London after Christmas!"Then Brent flashed her one of his cheesy smiles and exited the dorm's lobby.

Chapter Thirteen

Sometimes, just when you've hit your limits

Something comes along to

Bring you to the heart of the matter

Fortunately human beings have a

Limited number of neurons

Tune Reference: *King Of Pain*

----Police

CARIE NEVER MADE it as far as London.

"What is going on here? What about your scholarship?" Carrie's mother screamed without waiting for an explanation. "We'll talk about this when I get home." Then Carrie heard the click on the other end of the phone.

For several seconds Carrie remained frozen and then slowly replaced the receiver on the hook. Her mother's anger frightened her and Carrie could barely think. Responsible for her own college bill, the school had no reason to call her mother, who depended on Carrie on many levels. Without consulting her, some college authorities had left her no time to break the news to her mother gently. Carrie numbly gathered her things and called a taxi. Changing her departure date by several weeks, Carrie decided to leave on the next flight to Florida, part of the original plan that she shared with Brent. At a safe distance from the witch-hunt exploding on the Dallas campus, Carrie intended to confer with some friends in the warm climate.

When the taxi arrived Carrie hurriedly loaded her gear in the back and settled in the passenger seat.

"Airport," she instructed the woman driver who looked like she was still on the run.

The driver never required any further conversation and Carrie relaxed in the silence as the road-hardy station wagon sped along the airport freeway. *I've never felt so alive!* Carrie thought. I *may not know where I'm going, but at least I'm alive.* The woman across the seat smiled and nodded at Carrie, while the car accelerated through the traffic. Though the driver could not possibly hear Carrie's thoughts, she seemed to feel them.

When the vehicle passed Carrie's high school, she stole a final look at the campus. On the other side of the freeway stood the radio electronics store where Carrie had worked as a sales clerk last summer. As she left these memories behind, Carrie's thoughts sadly turned to the present circumstances.

Ever since the encounter with the Knights of Oblivion, her stamina had rapidly deteriorated. She quit eating regularly and lost too much weight for her athletic frame. Many of the things she learned in her classes added to the sick feeling in the pit of her stomach. The campus experienced an epidemic number of rapes after the incident involving the K of O and the authorities continued to deposit hardened criminals at the apartment complex across the street. The law-abiding students on campus voiced dissatisfaction with the university's denial of the security threats, and refused to take the necessary steps to protect its student population. This next step for the students involved being vigilantes and adopting guerrilla warfare, sorta like her neighborhood with Brian and the delinquents. Nobody, except the Viet Nam vet wanted to get caught hold the gun. Years ago, Carrie had made a similar choice to avoid confrontations with her father, who she would kill provoked into another confrontation. Her mother had sensed this, and compared her to the son in the movie *The Great Santini*. Having learned to walk away from machismo confrontations, Carrie never considered the notion that she would have to run from some places.

Before entering the university, her supervisor at the radio electronics store had cautioned her about the problems with sexual assault on the Rome campus. He knew several women who had attended the university and they had told him of their experiences there. Being in a foreign country, the women on campus had even greater difficulty in getting the university officials to address the problem. Carrie's future at the university appeared futile, as the professors refused to walk the talk of higher education. Her difficulty in regurgitating their fixed views for term papers had skyrocketed.

Carrie checked her baggage and walked through the smoky glass corridors towards the gate. As she anxiously stood in the area waiting to board her plane, Carrie gazed out the brown-colored windows enclosing the terminal. Yellow winter grass dotted the plains beyond the runway. The broad blue expanse in the sky promised her a safe flight from her former home. Once airborne, no one would be able to stop her until she landed at her destination. Pressing her face closer to the glass to hide from a policeman who walked by the terminal, Carrie suddenly recalled the incident with her mother which had hurt her so deeply a month after the assault.

Her cousin had almost died last semester from a collapsed lung. Instead of supporting her sister, her mother harangued Carrie when she came home to visit him in the hospital. The circumstances around his case became fodder for her mother's gossip. Always in the habit of blaming the victim, Carrie shouldered the false accusations that perhaps both of them drunk too much. Unable to toss off the verbal abuse as usual, Carrie quietly accepted her mother's ultimate decision: "No longer can you call this house your home anymore. You are like your father...you don't belong here with us."

To avoid being pressured into returning home or the university, Carrie hurried onto her plane when it arrived, hopping quickly into her seat. She knew that everything would be okay if she could just see the ocean again. The rolling waves would speak to her and remind her of how life goes on.

Her friend from high school seemed very happy to hear Carrie's voice on the phone. "Your mother called the police," she told her. "She thought that you might come and see me. The police have even been looking for you at the airport...Your mother worried that you might have killed yourself."

"Actually, she was going to kill me. I needed a break and some time to sort things through. I needed to see the ocean again," she admitted.

During the five days spent in Florida, Carrie stayed with the family of a college friend for a few days. Observing their interactions, she noticed how differently the family behaved from her own. They showed genuine concern and care for each other. Carrie felt so happy that she could have hugged the grocery store when they went shopping. She experienced the greatest joy in the most mundane activities—washing dishes, playing pool, shopping,...etc. Parallel to Carrie's conscious desire to see the ocean existed the unconscious burning of a single question: Was her idea of a loving family fact or fantasy? Like her visit to the ocean, she just had to know that it was there.

"You can't just disappear," her slightly obese high-school friend told Carrie. "Look at you, you're as skinny as a rail."

"Lean and mean," Carrie retorted, as she recalled her swim coach's favorite encouragements. She accepted the circumstances pertaining to her own family, when she began to feel drained by having spent too much time in one place. Carrie reluctantly returned to her mother's house by the end of the week.

Marty expressed surprise by Carrie's sudden departure. Feeling personally concerned, he met Carrie at her mother's house the same afternoon she arrived from the airport. During Carrie's absence Marty had spent many afternoons with Carrie's sisters at the house, waiting for news of Carrie's whereabouts. He fitted in well as an older brother and her sisters liked his company. They often invited him to stay for dinner, and Marty usually accepted their offer of a home-cooked meal.

After dinner that night, Marty and Carrie disappeared for a private stroll. "I sure am glad to see you," he started long after they had passed the first streetlight on the corner of the block. "You had me worried for a little while."

Having spent the last several minute walking quietly, Carrie paused a second when she heard his words. Still numb from his admission during the past summer, she didn't offer any sentiment. They turned the corner of the next block and continued down the paved road. Cars from the nearby highway roared softly in the background wind.

"You know, your youngest sister suspected that something was up all along," Marty continued, shaking his curly head at the pavement. "She said that you were too tired to play football with her over the holidays."

Carrie felt tears rush to her eyes, but she immediately took a deep breath and pushed them back. "I'm sorry I couldn't tell you. I didn't think you'd understand," she explained.

Marty stopped, looked Carrie directly in the eye, and cocked his head to one side. "Why did you think that I would not understand?" he stammered in frustration.

"Because you are a cynic and I'm an optimist, remember?" Carrie firmly replied without sadness or anger. Then she looked away at the distant blue stars shining in the black sky. The hint of a winter wind brushed her jacket, but months she felt as solid as the pavement, an impenetrable wall with a position as fluid as the sea waves in Florida. "I told you how rough things were going," Carrie reminded Marty when she returned his gaze. Then she paused for Marty's slow nod before continuing. "I have my dreams, my visions...these things I believe for my own sanity. I want something better for myself," she announced. "Nobody plays games on campus anymore. Playing soccer or football in the Mud Bowl lost its appeal, after the ceaseless attacks harbored by the fascists on campus. I cannot confide in someone who can't tell me they love me. That's just the way I am."

Marty and Carrie resumed walking. Without a word Marty looked sideways at her and nodded again; Carrie knew he understood now. Having made her point, she was glad Marty never told that he loved her that night.

Chapter Fourteen

Freedom requires

The ability to ride events out

Quickly

Tune Reference: *Ride Like The Wind*

----Christopher Cross

THE NEXT MORNING Carrie lingered in bed, waiting for her mother and youngest sister to leave for work and school. Carrie sighed, slumping back against the headboard. She had watched the lives of both her parents evolve through the years. As a very young girl, she had fingered the fresh scar that extended six inches across the base of their necks. Her mother claimed that the cut came from thyroid surgery, but Carrie never believed her mother.

As cloak and dagger operations continued to close around her, Carrie overheard her mother instructing Ellen to prevent her from leaving the house that day. Once she heard her mother's Oldsmobile roll down the driveway, Carrie hurriedly stretched across her bed to the front window and peered through an opening between the shutters. When Carrie saw the car make a quick right at the stop sign, her heart began its active beat and her eyes flickered open. She looked around her room and blinked. Despite her consciousness, the sense of numbness lingered.

Back in her room again, she felt the weight of her return bearing down on her as if she were a trapped animal. Like the shock of a captured rabbit, the jaws of an inevitable fate close around her. Accepting the mercy which with nature mysteriously compensates those who fall prey, Carrie became limp in her struggle at home to avoid being devoured by the pain she felt. She had come back from life to live with the dead.

Her thoughts were interrupted by the familiar sound of her cat, Cleo, forcing her way past the bedroom door. Bump! Squee-ea-ek! Bump! Soon Cleo arrived on top of the bed and met Carrie with a happy purr. The noise reminded Carrie of the good things in life which refused to change with time and events. The little Siamese cat assumed its favorite curl in Carrie's lap as Carrie ran her fingers over the soft fur. Cleo had already been out that morning because the black limbs of the cat's body felt cold. Automatically Carrie started warming the tips of Cleo's tiny ears with her hands as if she served as another cat licking life into her.

"Oh, Cleo!" she wept softly. The appearance of the little cat moved her. Many times she had dried her eyes with the black tip of Cleo's tail! "It's OK to cry now," she murmured so quietly that even Cleo couldn't hear. A stream of tears rushed down her face and landed on the cat. "Now Mom thinks I've been brainwashed," Carrie said, sadly shaking her head over the cat and feeling helplessly little inside. With a hint of chagrin, Carrie nuzzled the cat's head and added, "But, I think they brainwashed her a long time ago."

Shuddering at the thought of oblivion, Carrie shook the tension out of her body like an athlete keeping her muscles loose. She looked thoughtfully at Cleo, stroking the little cat's furry body. Although a house pet, Cleo possessed an independent mind. Oblivious to Carrie's woeful lament, the cat continued purring and nodding her wedge-shaped head in well-grounded euphoria. Carrie quieted as she watched the cat's response to her touch. In spite of her despair, the cat's ecstatic response amused her.

Evidently Cleo seemed amused by Carrie, so the relationship benefited them both. Carrie swept the cat into her arms, holding Cleo as tight as she could without harming the tiny beast. "You're just a bundle of love! You really don't know much of anything else," she agreed with the cat. "You're my lub-dub." Carrie rubbed her face against the cat's head and listened to the sounds of Cleo's existence: the purr, the breathing, the rapid thumping of Cleo's heart, the brushing noise of fur, whiskers, and skin. Carrie could find the beat of her own heart by listening to Cleo. Then Carrie released the cat into her lap and began absentmindedly drying her eyes with the black tip of Cleo's tail.

****

Carrie and her mother met Carrie's father at a psychiatrist's office later that afternoon. The moment the strain of the suspense became almost unbearable, Carrie's father emerged from the psychiatrist's office where daylight splashed the walls of the room from the windows on the western side. After adjusting her eyes to the light outside the waiting room, Carrie took a deep breathe and examined the office.

Propped up behind an enormous metal desk in a luxurious black sofa chair, sat a ruddy-faced platinum-haired woman. Everything else in the room seemed made out of glass or metal, and the only plant in the room, a spider plant hanging by the window, had begun to resemble the brown carpet below it. The woman's face reflected the luster of her objects, hardened by the displays of power decorating her office. Despite this, she appeared moved from the session with Carrie's father.

The psychiatrist glanced at Carrie as if she represented just another object and waved her to one of the insignificant chairs in the room. Frowning at her desk, the psychiatrist intently wrote more notes with the silver pen in her hand. The lack of direct eye contact gave Carrie the opportunity to settle into the sterile room without subtracting from the rigidity of its appearance. Once Carrie situated herself amongst the competing objects, the psychiatrist looked up from her notes and spoke. Without moving from her position behind the desk, the psychiatrist formerly introduced herself and explained that she wanted to ask Carrie a few questions.

"Did you say that you had a vision?" the psychiatrist began, after an introductory conversation.

"Well, yes," Carrie replied truthfully as the psychiatrist shook her head and wrote more notes. "It's sort of a inner vision, coming from my own imagination."

Carrie gulped, choosing to remain motionless in her chair. In spite of the consequences she opted to support her position on this matter. Whatever story her divorced parents gave the psychiatrist already had made a strong impression.

"Have you ever heard voices?" the psychiatrist persisted.

Hesitating a few seconds before answering this question, Carrie tried again, "They aren't voices as you might think. Sometimes I carry on dialogues in my head as if I am writing a play, sometimes I even coach myself, and sometimes the flashes of insight into a math or physics problem seem so certain that it is like a single voice."

Meanwhile, Carrie calmly noticed the lack of color in the passionless room. Any color which did exist seemed muted.

"Have you ever done drugs? Smoked pot?" the psychiatrist asked.

"Never. I hate drugs," Carrie told her. "I'm an athlete, and I don't like the side affects."

"Is it possible that anyone could have dropped some sort of drug in your drink or something?"

Carrie became more uneasy with the psychiatrist train of questions, which insinuated a conflict in value systems. Rather than be offended, Carrie inspected the psychiatrist's pinned perfect attire and silently questioned the psychiatrist's own personal habits.

"None of the people I hang out with do drugs," Carrie replied as she politely crossed her legs at the ankles. Any motion in the room now belonged as part of Carrie's statement.

"Why did you run away?" the psychiatrist finally questioned, shifting in her chair and looking away from her notes.

"I needed a vacation, a chance to get away from it all."

****

Two days after the meeting with the psychiatrist Carrie's mother deposited her at a city hospital. There they met Carrie's father who waited for them at the reception desk.

"It will just be for a week or two," both parents lied. "The doctor wants to run some tests. You'll be out in plenty of time for the Rome trip if you decide to go."

"Sign here on the dotted line," the admitting nurse instructed. Dressed in civilian clothes, only her name tag identified her affiliation with the hospital.

"It shows that you are mature enough to know when you need help," everyone coaxed.

Sitting down beside the reception desk, Carrie picked up a pen and studied the fine print at the end of the paper. Her left hand heavily brushed the bounce out of her hair as she thought. *Did she really have much of a choice?*

Looking up, Carrie read the faces of those who urged her to sign her life away and thought for a moment. At home Carrie's mother and sisters watched her every move, so that she'd be easily caught if she ever tried running away again. Where could she go now?

Chapter Fifteen

Never underestimate

The powers of creativity

Tune Reference: *Makin' Love Out Of Nothing At All*

----Air Supply

SCARCELY A WEEK after Carrie entered the hospital, another patient came to the ward. The new patient, a trim gentleman in his mid-forties endlessly paced the circular hall which joined all the rooms in the unit. The steadiness over some mighty question. His thinking processes were so focused that Carrie almost ran into him as she crossed the hallway from her room.

"Excuse me," he politely offered when Carrie searched his face for the meaning of his intense walk. The gentleman matched Carrie's glance and their eyes met. Looking deeply into his shiny almond-colored eyes, she found the omniscient spirit of a sea captain, an old salt who had skillfully guided his vessel through many of life's storms. Almost immediately a hurt shone through their strength, revealing their pain in a desperate plea for help. Without even daring to ask, the eyes called for human contact.

Carrie shyly looked at the floor. The handsome man had olive skin and distinguished lines of silver through his black hair. Sizing him up, she wondered, *how would a middle-aged man with such a square jaw accept anything she had to offer?* She looked at him again and her eyes caught the dark spot on his white turtleneck sweater. Although his attire indicated that he took pride in his appearance, he seemed like a waif in his present state. Carrie wished that he would put aside his quest long enough to care for himself. The man ignored her without denying his weakened state; some things were even more important than himself. He turned away abruptly and continued his journey around the hall.

"Who's that?" Carrie inquired as she met Eric, a teenage male four years her junior, just inside the door of the lounge.

"That's George," Eric answered, shaking his head in bewilderment. "I heard that he wants to get into alpha."

"Alpha?" Carrie murmured. Apparently alpha had landed George in the hospital.

"It's one of the mind's deepest levels of thinking," Eric explained solemnly.

Carrie pondered Eric's explanation for a few moments. Eric shook his head and looked at the floor. His face expressed deep concern for the older man. Remembering the desperation in the man's face, Carrie decided that she would help him if he ever approached her again.

Her opportunity arrived within the next few minutes. It appeared that George had heard her silent thoughts, because he entered the lounge on his next turn around the ward. Carrie stopped chatting with Eric and his friends and turned towards George. He approached the group, attempting to articulate a question, but his deep thoughts proved too difficult to verbalize. Then he motioned the teenagers towards a chalkboard on the wall where he could communicate in writing. The adults in the room moved away to the opposite end of the room, feeling uncomfortable with George's inability to speak and hopeless gestures.

Carrie stood at the man's left shoulder as she watched him pick up a piece of chalk with his right hand. He examined the chalk with a slight smile, wielding the powerful communication tool that was now in his grasp. This writing instrument would be the key to his thoughts. Raising his arm over writing before making a mark. For a few seconds he made circular motions in the air until he connected the motion of the chalk in his hand to the motion of thoughts within his head. Then he glanced sideways at Carrie to be sure that she still paid attention. Carrie quietly nodded her readiness before George quickly glanced at Eric who stood on his right side. Encouraged that his attempt in communication would not be in vain, George commenced with the yellowed chalk.

He drew a slow, careful white oval against the blackness of the board. "How can an egg be a triangle?" he asked, finally finding the words.

Briefly, Carrie stepped back and wondered whether she should censored her answer. Accustomed to such questions in her philosophy, physics, and calculus classes as overpaid, frenzied professors wildly lined the board in a few seconds. Clearly, the difference became a matter of circumstance. Some people paid good money to puzzle over devices called rubik's cubes. Compared to their ranting and raving, George appeared rather sane. He also seemed more sensitive to his audience.

Feeling encouraged, she picked up a piece of chalk and drew a possible derivation on the board. In the tradition of western thought, the triangle illustrated the three different aspects of a single entity: body, mind, and spirit. Generally the symbol was used in a male context of father, son, and spirit. Likewise, the egg could represent a female version of how three distinct parts formed a single entity like the parts of an egg: yolk, white, and shell.

"See it fits inside easily," she observed, rounding the egg inside the triangle she had drawn. "It touches all the sides." Besides female maturity, the circle symbolized continuity between alpha and omega, the beginning and the end.

Doug, a lanky seventeen-year-old male standing at the far corner of the board, proposed his own drawings to Carrie when she stepped back to double-check her figures. He suggested the biological symbols for male and female. Carrie blushed at his overt flirtation, politely shaking her head at the hot-blooded philosopher. He had a good point, though sex didn't always result from biology or religious necessity.

Wishing to incorporate some romantic chemistry between the biological symbols, Carrie considered some figures which could relate more freely to the other. It bothered her that the triangle must conform to the size of the enclosed circle for the sides to touch. The circle, on the other hand, seemed constrained by the size of the triangle. So Carrie drew a strong and wide O on the board. Such a nice O, Carrie believed, deserved a big strong 1. After completing her 1 as handsomely as she could, Carrie studied the two figures together. The desire between the two figures seemed very natural and strong. In fact, the desire for the other form appeared so strong that the figures sought each other.

Satisfied with her answer, Carrie left the board, separating herself from the group while leaving her answer intact. George smiled and waved his hand at Carrie as he stayed at the board with the male teenagers. Carrie nodded back and left the lounge to return to her room for the night, still contemplating her latest drawing. Mostly, she thought, George just wanted someone to listen and relate to him.

Because Carrie's therapist generally discouraged interaction with the other patients, Carrie's schedule prevented her from seeing George and the others until a week later. Meanwhile, the psychiatrist increased Carrie's medication, severely impairing Carrie's motor functions. Carrie spent her spare moments recuperating from the effects of the drugs, lying painfully sprawled across the bed in her room. One drug, known by the patients as the roller coaster, compelled Carrie to run out of her skin one minute and made her drowsy the next minute. Another drug immobilized her, while creating a trembling in her limbs so heavy that she exercised all motions with extreme caution. Carrie felt like crying every time she noticed the shaking in her hands, a sharp contrast to the graceful forms she created with her dives. Imprisoned, now she watched the doctors destroy her.

As a result of the medication, Carrie felt very sick and tired when she visited the lounge again. This time she spotted George, Eric, Doug, and some of the others sitting at a table across the room. George raised his hand and smiled at Carrie. He wore a clean shirt and seemed very alert as he chatted animatedly with those around him. On his right sat a very attractive olive-skinned woman with deep dark eyes. The beautiful woman, apparently George's wife, sparkled brightly at Carrie and whispered to George, "Is this the one? She's beautiful!"

For a few seconds Carrie beamed with the woman's approval. Then she stared sadly at the hospital floor while measuring the painful effects of the hospital on her body. Not the time nor the place to encourage friendships or develop attachments, Carrie downplayed her interaction with the others Declining the invitation to join the group, Carrie chose a nearby chair in a quiet corner of the room. There she read her book, while keeping her ears tuned to the conversation at the table. She wanted George to concentrate on leaving the hospital.

In the days that followed George used his talents as an executive salesman to make the hospital a better place. He successfully captured the ear of the head nurse and organized a committee to voice patient grievances and protect their rights. Because of his persuasiveness, the hospital installed an air filter in the lounge to clean up the cigarette smoke. Carrie admired his courage and learned from his diplomatic style as he voiced his concerns over the head nurse's patronizing responses. He became Carrie's silent champion and Carrie wished that someday she would be able to do the same about the things which concerned her.

Another woman who entered the ward only a few days after George proved as equally vocal as George about patient rights. This woman hid in the hospital to avoid being killed by someone who had threatened her life. The woman owned a supply store and had aroused the wrath of some man she refused business. This woman and George became fast friends and Carrie quietly enjoyed their company whenever she made it into the patient lounge. Although she felt too physically sick to ever participate in the rapport, she always sat close enough to listen and watch.

One day, while Carrie waited to speak with one of the nurses at the nurse's station about the increased dosages the psychiatrist prescribed for her, Carrie spotted her patient chart lying opened on the near desk. Skimming the contents, Carrie learned that the section had been written by the portly male nurse on the day of the chalkboard drawings. Although the male nurse professed to be a born-again-christian, the references to John the Baptist in the chart surprised her. Appalled by his poetic license, Carrie surmised that the patients remained at the mercy of the staff's fantasies.

As a result of her revelation Carrie maintained discrete contact with George, Doug, and some of the others. They followed her cue and immediately realized the hostile situation. They began accepting the roles given to them by the hospital staff like actors and actresses to save their real spiritual identities from scrutiny and oppression. George's physicians released him within two weeks. The other woman left two days later. Despite the lack of direct contact, Carrie wept after George and the woman left.

Though happy to see them leave the hospital, she missed their warmth very much. As the effects of the drugs became more pronounced with each passing week, Carrie learned more about how the psychiatrist and therapist viewed her case. Nobody had spoken to her about what to expect in terms of hospital therapy and Carrie became lost in the environment, living patiently from one day to the next without any apparent reason for remaining there. After having stayed at the hospital for a month, the therapist gave her a few clues.

"Historically, every culture has its list of topics which are treated as taboo," the counselor from Argentina lectured in her thick German accent. As she listened to the therapist's lengthy discourse, Carrie rummaged through the corners of her mind for an appropriate reply. The effect of the drugs heavily bound Carrie to the chair like chained weights and she had difficulty focusing. She carefully eyed the therapist in front of her, one of the people presently responsible for making her life so miserable and painful that she scarcely had the energy to remember how to read or write, much less remember her life before the hospital. Finally, Carrie realized the reason for the lack of direct communication concerning her case; she had emerged as the taboo subject, the skeleton in someone's closet.

When the therapist finished, Carrie offered a taboo subject instead of herself. "A long time ago, when I was six or seven, I found an injured baby blue jay in the backyard. Some kids from the other side of the fence claimed that the bird belonged to them and that they were taking care of it. After I gave the bird away my mother came outside. She hit me for handing the bird over to the older children on the other side of the fence."

Carrie paused for a moment to wipe away a tear. Then she softly explained, "My mother told me that mother birds kill the baby birds that are touched by humans. She told me that the baby bird would die because I had touched it."

Then Carrie glanced at the therapist for her response. Failing to make the connection between the past and present circumstances, the therapist murmured something incoherent and stared at the floor. A few seconds later, the therapist looked up, handed Carrie a tissue in a token gesture to wipe away the tears Carrie had incurred during the moment, and eagerly began writing in the chart book. Without bothering to dry her eyes, Carrie held the tissue in her hands, determining whether the therapist would require anymore tears from her.

Chapter Sixteen

Any which way you slice it

Abuse is abuse

Tune Reference: *Psychobabble*

----The Alan Parsons Project

THE MONTHS SLOWLY passed in the hospital while the details concerning the intent of Carrie's therapy remained vague. The psychiatrist failed to choose a diagnosis for Carrie and had even greater difficulty dealing with her parents. Accepting her weakened state, she concentrated on those activities which appeared innocuous to the hospital staff. Carrie devised many ways to entertain herself behind the closed walls. She played her guitar in the lounge for the others and went walking or jogging whenever she could obtain a pass to go outside. She learned how to crochet and tried all sorts of artistic endeavors during the open hours of the art room. These activities enabled Carrie to tune out the more obnoxious patients and hospital staff.

"This place is just like a WWII concentration camp," a portly male yelled at several of the nurses in the ward. Then he remarked to those inside the art room, "The staff are like Nazi guards and the patients are the prisoners."

"Do we need to ask the doctors to increase your medication?" threatened the head nurse, a blond possessing the same facial luster as the psychiatrist in the metallic office.

Carrie dropped the paint brush she used and switched to a thicker one. Usually this chubby middle-age man chattered about his sexual preference for pre-adolescent males. She noted that he had made progress in recovering from his own control issues. After her second month in the hospital, Carrie started treating most of the hospital staff as stooges from Soviet gulags, and ironically they responded by showing her greater respect. They probably never would have realized how she really felt about their abusive need for power, but their unconscious response exposed their complicity. Turning the sword directed at her around into a double-edged sword, she observed them as much as they watched her. Carrie mastered a philosophical approach to the situation and just continued to feed their plays as if they were caged animals in a zoo.

She tilted her head back and critically eyed her acrylic painting. At least now she had time to paint; she had sorely missed the activity while a pressured, college student. This present painting showed signs of recovering from the initial shock of being in the hospital. Initially, the trees in her landscapes looked like something a two year old might paint. As much as she tried she failed to correct the perspective, until she started treated the staff like gulag stooges. Having mastered the art of escaping the hospital system for her benefit, her artwork regained its former sophistication. Carrie chose another brush and blended more colors on her wooden canvas while the head nurse and Bill quietly argued in the hall.

Another patient rushed into the art room. "The boy is gone! He escaped again!" She whispered excitedly. This slightly mentally-retarded woman who had been abused by her mother, grandparents, and medical professionals, admired the high school escapee. "I helped him the last time," she boasted, "...when he hid inside the lunch cart and the staff wheeled downstairs to the kitchen."

After surprising the bewildered kitchen workers, the teenage male quickly jumped out of the cart and bolted out of the hospital. The nineteen-year-old all-American boy, had been hospitalized for attempting suicide after his girlfriend broke up with him. His first escape consisted of dashing past the male nurses when someone opened the metal door to the ward. In this second escape, Cory hid in a lunch cart going back to the kitchen. After the fire department found him hiding in an abandoned field, they stripped off his clothes and locked him in isolation.

"He just popped a ceiling tile and tried crawling out over our heads during group session," the mentally-retarded woman continued. "The fire department is chasing him inside the crawl space now."

Two hours later, Carrie watched the fully-clothed youth jubilantly stroll into the patient lounge. "They are going to let me go home," he announced.

This time the hospital decided against imposing any punitive measures. The young boy sat down in the rocking chair beside Carrie and excitedly rocked. "My Dad is buying me a car. My buddies and I are taking it on test drive to New Orleans next weekend...can't wait to see how it does on the highway."

Carrie nodded, knowing that the boy's father took delighted pride in his son's hospital escapes.

Then the teenage boy shook his head and stared at the floor between his knees. "No girl is worth committing suicide over. Nobody is worth that much."

Staring wistfully at the distant wall, Carrie sensed, though, that the girl served as only part of the reason for the suicide attempt. His actions reminded her of the value of freedom, and Carrie felt compelled to assume minor risks for her own sense of human dignity. Eying a hardback edition of

Graham Greene's *Comedians* tucked inconspicuously among the random assortment of paperback love novels, she reached for the book and took it back to her room. Opening the book on the desk, she hid her crochet needle underneath, so that staff would not take it away, claiming that she might use it to kill herself.

With a grin, she developed immunity from the soap operas traumatizing the inhabitants. The book said more about the comic routines of the author, who had aided Castro under auspices of British intelligence and Catholic church. From everything that she had witnessed at the university, the notion of Professor MetaFist and his anti-US escapades matched Greene's depiction of business as usual underneath Spanish derivatives. Eventually, she concocted a poem, which wrapped her therapists in their own nonsensical beliefs and valueless constructs. The older patients applauded her poem, whereas the staff merely froze, lost in the same blue haze that swirled Greene to his ineffectual ends.

Within weeks, the hospital finally discharged Carrie on the conditions that she never return to either of her parents' homes and continue therapy as an outpatient. Carrie had stayed at the hospital for four months, much longer than the two-week agreement. The psychiatrist had become a third party in the bitter power struggles between her divorced parents, similar to the one dividing Greene and the US over Cuba.

Although she found a job and a place to stay, Carrie returned to her mother's house a week after her release. In making the transition from the prison of the hospital to the civilian world, Carrie realized that she needed something familiar. Her mother and sisters wanted her home to celebrate Easter.

Chapter Seventeen

Maybe...

Tune Reference: *Maybe It's You*

----Words by John Bettis and music by Richard Carpenter

INITIALLY, CARRIE'S RELATIONSHIP with her family went smoothly, as the overt domestic abuse ceased for the moment. Eager to become self-sufficient as well as minimize her family contact, she immediately found work as a grocery store cashier which paid very well. She assumed a second job at the community college where she earned nine credit hours during the summer. Though the college work study position didn't pay as much as grocery store business, Carrie enjoyed the comradery that the print shop offered.

Meanwhile, she severed relations with the university, maintaining friendships with only a few close individuals. Most of Carrie's classmates thought that she had simply dropped out of school, except for one student who pursued her sudden disappearance.

On a midsummer's afternoon she received a phone call from Brent, her head-to-head conversationalist from the campus blood drive. He greeted in a familiar voice, "Hi, this is BW!"

"BW?" Carrie answered, perplexed by the familiar sounding voice.

"Brent Wright," he rejoined. "BW is a nickname."

"Oh...," Carrie said slowly as she quickly connected the name and face to the sender of some mystery letters that had been sent to her home.

"I missed you in Europe. How are you doing?" BW asked.

"Oh, I'm doing alright. I landed in the hospital and had to cancel the trip to Rome."

"I'm sorry to hear that," he said quietly. "I've tried calling you, but I had to look up the number in the phone book. There are quite a few of you with the same last name. I called most of them. Did you get the letters I sent?"

"Yes, I did. Thank you very much. I'm a rough go of it and wasn't in much of a position to respond."

"I'm glad to hear that you're doing much better." Changing the subject, Brent simply asked, "Would you like to see the musical *My Fair Lady* this Saturday?"

"That's the one starring Rex Harrison...," Carrie commented while weighing the possibility of dating someone else besides Marty. The friendly voice at the other end of the wire touched Carrie with its sincerity. Impressed that he had tracked down her phone number. Carrie decided, "Yes, Saturday sounds fun."

Brent arrived Saturday afternoon. Assuming the role of hostess, her youngest sister opened the front door and invited Brent into the house as Carrie finished dressing. Donning a cool cotton tan dress for the summer night, she reviewed the worst shaving job in her entire life. Nervous about getting out again, she hid the red marks on her legs with flesh-colored hose. Then she hurriedly fastened her feet into a comfortable pair of dress sandals and ran to save Brent from her family's scrutiny.

"How are you doing, lady?" Brent said elegantly, meeting Carrie with a smile.

Without hesitation, Carrie looked directly into his eyes and noticed a few tears welding inside their blueness. Surprised by his concern, she sat down on the couch before the trembling in her legs betrayed her giddiness. Taken aback by his respectful terms of endearment, she composed herself quietly without answering. Noting the absence of his Greek sailor's cap, Carrie studied Brent's formal attire of plaid slacks and shiny yellow shirt. He dressed in same the harmonious fashion as an artist displaying his paintings. Admiring his appearance for the sensual maturity it projected, Carrie looked forward to spending more time with Brent.

Together they left the house. Stepping down from the front porch, Brent directed Carrie to a functional pile of metallic junk parked in the driveway. "Meet Maxwell," he said as if introducing her to a roommate.

"Maxwell, the physicist?" Carrie grinned, giving the bug a second look as she considered the impact on the neighboring pretensions. With a shrug, she admitted that it matched the comedy show of the hospital imprisonment.

"Ya, the one responsible for the famous Maxwell equations in electromagnetic theory," he said as they got into the car and began the forty-minute drive to the city music hall. "My father and I picked out two VW bugs at the local auto yard," Brent explained as he sped over the highway. "We plan to convert them to solar power. My father found the plans in a magazine and sent away for them. The car can be built from a VW chassis. One guy managed to drive his solar powered bug over the Rockies. He stopped every two hours to let the batteries recharge."

Having never even considered building a solar powered car, Carrie carefully, she examined the insides of Maxwell while contemplating the intricacies of such an undertaking. Then she noticed the handmade wooden knobs on the doors, glove box, and stick shift.

"My dad made those," Brent interjected proudly, observing her curiosity. "I made the one on the glove box that keeps falling off," Brent explained while reaching across the car to demonstrate. Carrie anxiously glanced at Maxwell's swerve on the highway. Regaining control of the vehicle, he continued, "I need to glue it in place. My dad has a shop in the basement. The original handles were broken so we just whittled some new ones."

"I like the workmanship. What else do you make?"

"Most everything. We make our own butter, soap, applesauce, cider, vinegar, wine...Daddy tried making champagne once, but it had too much fizz. He produced two cases worth. Of the twenty-four bottles of champagne: the first cork put a hole in the kitchen ceiling, twenty corks cleared the telephone wires outside, and the remaining three bottles exploded in the basement."

Carrie looked at Brent with amazement. She had been raised on instant cake mixes and homogenized milk.

"How did you learn to do these things?" she asked.

"My father raised us on a farm. He and Mom bought an old farmhouse with ten acres the year after they married. He learned about running a farm by trial and error. He also works as a test engineer for an aircraft company. On vacations he loves to go fly fishing."

Gazing at the dry, yellowed hills, she commented, "There's not much fly fishing around here. We do a lot of pole fishing." She offered, "My high school chemistry instructor and I wanted to paint our lures with glow-in-the-dark paint. I found the recipe to make fluorescent calcium sulfite in a chemistry book. It makes glow-in-the-dark paint." Hesitating a moment to be sure she had Brent's attention, Carrie continued, "I crushed some oyster shells, mixed the powder with sulfur, and heated the mixture in an old butter dish while the family was away. The hood above the stove collected the fumes and the experiment went along fine. However the stuff wouldn't glow. My instructor and I tried the experiment at school, and the results were the same. Evidently, the oyster shells didn't contain enough impurities. It's the barium and zinc impurities that cause the stuff to glow.

"We'd consider that cheating," Brent challenged with a grin as the wind from a small side window tousled his curly, dark hair. "Fly fishermen just use a hook. The secret is in the wrist motion of the cast; it makes fishing a real sport...and you must fall in the stream at least once, otherwise you can't consider it a real fishing trip," he added while adjusting the window' opening to save his hairstyle.

"I'll have to try that some time. There's little opportunity around here she replied. Leaving Brent speechless for a brief moment, Carrie ignored the healthy wind currents rocking the Volkswagon and proceeded with another topic. "There's something I've been meaning to ask you...," Carrie started. "Are you the same BW who sent the photo and letter to my Mom last fall?"

"Ya, that was me," he said with a proudly smile. "Should have seen the photos of my friend and his girlfriend that I sent to his parents. It consisted of a series of shots with the last frame showing his girlfriend sitting on his lap. His parents loved it, and so did my friend. They wrote me a really nice letter. Other parents who received photos wrote me also. Parents like to hear how their sons and daughters are doing away from home. It's a lot of fun and it makes many people very happy. My job with the yearbook gives me access to the addresses of all the parents."

Carrie searched the innocent face of the mystery writer and swallowed hard, imagining her mother's alarm in contrast to other's appreciation. She never bothered telling him that her mother disliked the letter, being suspicious of an any outsider's interest. Declining to complicate

Brent's world, she humored him. For the remainder of the evening, Carrie let Brent do most of the talking. She listened to his version of the world, which brought a smile to his face. By the time that the musical ended, she smiled with him.

The following week Carrie invited Brent on a hike and picnic at one of her favorite nearby lakes. The trails changed seasonally and she enjoyed staying in tune with the changes in the same manner one maintains contact with a friend. According to the amount of rainfall received each month, the lake would redistribute its waters with respect to the varying topography. Every time she visited the site Carrie always discovered something new and different in the lake's biosphere. The quick recovery of the terrain corresponded with its ability to accept change. Carrie noticed that nature often compensated with the dramatic growth of certain species of wildlife and vegetation which restored the biosphere. Watching the continuity of these cycles in the web of life inspired Carrie with a sense of connection.

Today she took Brent to this environment. Carrie led the way over the winding green trails as Brent and she hopped over tiny streams and scurried through gullies to the music of croaking frogs and chirping crickets. Brent toted his camera around his neck and occasionally tried enticing Carrie to pose for a few snapshots. She discouraged him by directing attention to their surroundings.

After feeling a raindrop brush her face, Carrie stopped abruptly and peered at the darkening sky. "Brent, do you feel any raindrops?" she asked while testing for the droplet amount with her palm extended to the sky. No sooner had Carrie spoken, then a flurry of water bombarded them. This spray forewarned the advent of a summer storm, the kind that could bring every kid in Carrie's neighborhood outside to swim in the torrential street gutters.

She watched Brent's face for an expression of his feelings; they were both waiting for the other to decide on a course of action. She quickly assumed the initiative, "I think that we should make our way back to the car. There's no telling how long this downpour will last and I'm cold."

Minutes later, hail the size of popcorn pelted them from the clouds and rain poured in buckets. The tiny streams Brent and Carrie had crossed earlier reached the full extent of their gullies, forcing them to create a new route to the car. Brent followed closely behind her. Carrie appreciated the trust in her capabilities. Most men she knew would have insisted on carving the route to the car themselves, regardless of their unfamiliarity with the area. These macho rituals escaped Brent, who seemed more advanced for the moment.

While they wandered through the mud and blinding rain, Brent reached out and placed his Greek sailor's cap on her head. "Wear this," he instructed. "You're getting chilled; I can see the goose bumps on your arms...a person loses ninety percent of their body heat through the head."

Accepting his advice, Carrie grinned and adjusted the cap. Not only did she have his trust, but she presently sported one of his most prized possessions. She turned around and continued the journey as the rain transformed into a light sprinkle. When Brent and Carrie reached the car, they ignored the vehicle and decided against canceling the picnic. While dark clouds hurried across the sky, Brent and Carrie basked in the intermittent sun bursts. The sun's warmth penetrated the sopping dampness of their hiking clothes and dried their skin after the showers ceased. Brent and Carrie loitered on a series of nearby rocks where Brent stole a few photographs of her. This time Carrie submitted to the whims of his photographic art. The summer storm had removed their awkwardness. They found a dry spot underneath the swaying branches of a weeping willow for their picnic. As they relaxed and chatted over the assortment of food in the picnic basket, Carrie looked at Brent for what seemed to be the first time. A veil of guise fell from between them. She observed the man before her as if she had a pair of new eyes. He wore jogging shorts and a tank top which revealed wiry muscles on his lean frame. Brent brightened as if he could sense her silent appraisal. His slow deliberate actions nourished her admiration, calling further attention to his form. When she realized that Brent had been observing the subtle movements of her own body, Carrie became conscious of her own motions. Silently she nodded with the realization of the attraction between them.

Brent took her home later in the afternoon where Carrie said goodbye and hugged him warmly on the porch steps. No longer just a guy from college, he represented a friend. He accepted Carrie's embrace with a gentle smile and returned to his mechanical pal, Maxwell, for the drive back to his apartment.

Chapter Eighteen

When you find yourself

Entering the circle

Get out

Tune Reference: *Valley Of The Dolls*

----Alan Jay Lerner and Burton Lane

A FEW DAYS later Carrie visited the therapist, according to their agreement. In a thick German accent, she lectured Carrie on sexual freedom and told her to have intercourse with Marty. Stunned by her aggression, Carrie backed off the subject.

"I broke up with him a few days ago," Carrie admitted.

"Oh you did...," the therapist commented, while scrutinizing Carrie's face for the justification.

"I wanted to make a clean break," Carrie explained as she squirmed uncomfortably in her chair. She knew that the therapist would not understand her relationship with Marty, so she quickly drew the therapist's attention to a more pertinent problem. "There's something else..." Carrie began as her hands sought the letter inside her purse that she had received from Brent only a day ago. She shook her head over the letter, running her right hand over the top of her forehead. "I have another problem. The letter is from Brent, the friend from school who sent me all those letters that I never answered. He's the one who looked me up when he returned from Rome." Carrie sighed heavily. "Now he says he loves me. He even signed it that way."

Putting the folded letter away by her side, Carrie announced, "I don't think I should see him anymore." Gazing at the heavy metallic items in the therapist's office, Carrie could not forget that the arrangement between the two of them had been by force. She thought about the impact that Brent's cutesy love letter would have on all their psychological evaluations. *Would it undermine the nurse's fantasy about John the Baptist?* Her mother had wanted her to believe that nobody loved her for years.

"Why?" the therapist demanded in her thick accent.

"There's something wrong about it. I don't understand his letter. This guy must be strange or something."

"May I read it?" the therapist asked, her curiosity aroused. Carrie immediately handed the letter over, feeling relieved to get it off her hands. The therapist devoured its substance. Finishing, she leaned back in her chair and grinned with her eyes half closed. "He loves you."

"He what?" Carrie stared at her in disbelief. "Are you sure?" she gulped.

"Read the letter again!" She instructed, tossing the letter on Carrie's lap.

Carrie skimmed over the words, and played *Comedian*. "Well, what do you know?" Then she gasped, "But what about the hospital? It's not so good to fall in love with me," she whispered as tears welled inside her eyes.

"I think you should tell him. He already knows something is up," the therapist reminded her.

True, Carrie thought, weighing the Argentine-German's advice carefully.

The woman leaned back in her chair again and took a long drag off the skinny cigarette. She nodded until Carrie agreed with her.

Carrie straightened in her chair with the advice, resuming her composure. Then she thanked her and left. After the meeting with the therapist Carrie went home and called Brent that same evening. She invited Brent over for the following afternoon, telling him that she needed to talk with him about something important. Brent accepted her invitation, happily promising Carrie his ready assistance on any matter which concerned her.

When he arrived the next day, Carrie answered his knock on the front door and ushered him into the living room where she had arranged a plate of brownies. She had chosen a time when she knew her mother and sisters would be absent from the house for a few hours, away from hearing distance.

"Have some brownies," Carrie offered as they sat down on the living room sofa. Having heard that the quickest way to reach Brent's heart was through his stomach, Carrie desperately wanted to take full advantage of the effect. She watched in delight as Brent eagerly picked up a couple of brownies from the plate.

"Would you like some milk?" Carrie asked, disappearing into the kitchen before Brent answered.

"That would be wonderful!" he exclaimed, standing up after her. Carrie glanced at the enthusiastic skinny frame waiting for her in the living room. He seemed willing to digest anything she divulged.

She joined him in the living room and handed him a glass of milk to accompany the brownie that he held in his hand. Slowly they resumed their former seats on the sofa as Carrie started, "Brent, there are a few things I need to tell you."

Brent sipped his milk for a few seconds and then politely placed the glass on the coffee table. "What is it, lady?" he asked, moving his body closer to hers.

Surprised that the brownies could produce such dramatic results, Carrie backed away from his approach, before continuing, "Well, you know the city hospital?...My parents put me in there because I ran away."

Brent protectively placed his arm around Carrie, demonstrating his refusal to be scared away by her information. Carrie remained motionless underneath his arm and explained further, "The hospital said that I would need medication for the rest of my life, sorta like the fluoride peppered in the water to send the Jews off to the concentration camps."

True to the spirit of a male protector, Brent straightened and lightly squeezed Carrie. "It's alright," he assured her. "I'm on your side."

Carrie disregarded his knightly offer. "Thanks for your support," she answered without returning his embrace. She sighed as her gaze fell to the table with the brownies and milk."There's something else...I'm not sure if I'm up for the astronomy party at the university. You never know who some of these people hang out with after hours, and I might get hurt. Not everyone sees it through my eyes."

"If there is anything I can do to make it easier on you, let me know," he offered. For some reason Carrie felt that she could trust Brent's words and she let him take her hand in his. His manner suggested that he represented the heartfelt concern of many of people on campus.

Weeks later, Brent offered his own confession. Having agreed to go on an errand with him, he asked her to sit down in a plush chair in the office. He explained further in voice which was barely audible, "There's something I want to tell you."

Now it was her turn to listen to his story. Surprised by his announcement, Carrie looked up at Brent from the assortment of papers and magazines which had caught her eye, unsure what to expect next, but the expression on Brent's face told her that it was a very serious matter. "I dated some other girls while I stayed in Rome," he began gravely, "and became involved in some heavy necking with one of them."

Brent paused in his confession, heaving a weighted sigh. "I regretted it afterwards, feeling that I had gone too far. I didn't intend to become so physically involved, but it just sorta happened. I promised myself that it wouldn't ever happened again," he told Carrie, shaking his head over his self-imposed guilt.

Offering no comment, Carrie cautiously maintained her silent ear. She knew of Brent's former affairs in the campus fishbowl, and doubted that the savvy beauty entertained the same sexual mores. Brent continued, "One of the things I look for in a girlfriend is the nurturing instinct. It's important for me ideal of mine very closely." Brent stopped speaking for a few seconds and looked directly at Carrie. "I just want you to know that...I've never met anyone like you. Whether you realize it or not, you have all the qualities of a good mother. I can see it from your interactions with people."

Carrie met Brent's eyes, nodding at his forwardness as he quickly pushed his glasses back on his nose. Ignoring his guilt, she simply shrugged in response. Many people on campus worshipped madonnas and virgins; the various departures from the iconic versions remained a matter of personal preference.

The next week the psychiatrist phoned Carrie to apologize for the therapist's sudden departure to Argentina. Carrie sighed with relief, finally able to get out of paying the bill for someone to pry into her love life. Carrie seized the opportunity to drop herself from the psychiatrist's list of cases, and agreed to one trial visit.

When the psychiatrist pressured her at the next visit, Carrie shook her head, and played the card that therapist's departure had ruined everything. Nonetheless, the psychiatrist persevered, "Your father gave me some information about you that you don't know. You need to stay with me."

Familiar with her father's smooth-talking ways with women, Carrie stood up to the psychiatrist. "I didn't like the drugs that you put me on in the hospital and I didn't like the way my father treated me. I have decided to move on."

Blushing, the therapist turned in her swivel chair and threatened, "You'll need to know it later in life."

With that answer, Carrie shook her head and left the room before the visit went into overtime. She wrote the receptionist a final check and walked out a free woman, at least for most of the summer.

Throughout the summer Carrie continued her studies at a community college and worked two jobs. One job, checking groceries at a local supermarket, enabled Carrie to earn a substantial sum of money in a relatively short amount of time. Despite the high wages, almost one half of the hired checkers quit .seem to affect Carrie and she obtained a second job in the print shop at the community college. Although everyone in the print shop was a hard worker, they made time for practical jokes and watermelon picnics. Carrie blended well with the people at the print shop, and they taught her many things about the bindery and printing business. By the end of the summer, Carrie had saved enough money to realize one of her immediate goals: getting a car.

"It's your color," her mother commented when she saw the blue Toyota two-door.with the color blue. At least, not anymore. Carrie had chosen the car for its performance and the smooth running engine tucked neatly underneath the car's hood; exterior color had been an unimportant issue in her mind. Carrie sighed deeply and looked at the gray cement driveway underneath the car's wheels. She knew that driveway like she knew her own bed, having spent many hours lying on her back to repair the cars parked above her. Carrie had been worried that her mother might become upset and encourage her to immediately get rid of the vehicle. Any move Carrie made for greater self-reliance or independence never seemed well-received at home.

Carrie kept the car, focusing on the many features that she really liked about the automobile. She enjoyed listening to the tape deck and zipping the car's sleek body around turns and into parking spaces. Excited about the feel of the wheel in her hands, Carrie drove the car to the community college during the following week. Usually, she rode her bike, but Carrie wanted to utilize the commute time for joy-riding in her car. Lately, she had been spending her spare moments catching up on her sleep. She always felt tired these days, and she wanted to take the car on a pleasure trip when she had enough energy to make it a pleasant one.

Pulling into a space in the landscaped parking lot at the community college, Carrie quickly turned off the engine and leaned back against her seat. She took a deep breath as she glanced above at one of the thickly leafed trees shading the car. Shaking her head, Carrie felt the heat of the sun melt her into the car's blueness. It would be awhile before she found the strength to resume bicycling the six mile distance to campus in the 100 degree temperatures.

With her mother's words resounding in her ears, Carrie realized the futility of her efforts in trying to ever escape—the heat, the exhaustion, the dark blue...All these thoughts jumbled through her, leading to deeper revelations. Her efforts to escape the conditions of her past and home environment appeared futile and senseless. Desperately, she wanted to touch the fun and exciting people she had encountered through work and school, but her past hospitalization marred her like a growing blue ink stain on a white shirt. Her eyes measured the amount of freedom in the steering wheel before it caught the safety lock. Click. The wheel no longer moved. The degree of freedom proved minimal.

Several days later, Carrie feigned a suicide attempt and started scratching her left wrist, until her youngest sister retrieved her mother.

"Carrie, I'll get you some good help," her mother said in her most soothing voice. "A friend of mine has a husband who takes the same medication that you do. He really likes his doctor. Says that he's the best in the city. This time we'll get you some good help."

Then she left and Carrie overheard her make a few phone calls. Still feeling lightheaded, Carrie blinked her eyes and looked blankly at her bedroom. That evening Carrie's mother drove her to a place which had been open for a month. Operated by a young, innovative graduate from Stanford who approached medical problems from a biological standpoint. Immediately, the clinic took Carrie off all medication and ran a series of blood tests. After a month of tests and observations they put her on thyroid medication. The doctor hypnotized her before she left and said that she could always through herself in a trance when needed.

I usually decline to comment on the practices of my colleagues in the medical profession, but the treatment you received is deplorable," The doctor told Carrie after a month. "The medication they gave you adversely affected your biological system and possibly caused the hypothyroidism that you are experiencing now. Your EEGs are normal, and the CAT scan appeared normal.

Brent had called Carrie at the clinic after the first week. He had recently returned from a trip and wanted to talk to her. He had been visiting a female classmate from the university. She neglected telling him about the circumstances of her admission to the clinic, and Brent never asked for details. Brent visited her almost every day. Often he'd bring Carrie letters and cards from some of her friends at the university. Carrie looked forward to Brent's visits and always thanked him. Gradually he won her trust through his devotion. Step by step, Carrie weaved her way out of the system and agreed to work for her mother's boyfriend. When his son sexually pressured her, she hurried through the welding. Unsatisfied, or feigning dissatisfaction with the results, the boyfriend asked her to not come back. Though she left a trail of frustrated tears, she found a waitress job close to home. When her mother pressured her to see the clinic doctor again, Carrie painted pictures and relied on art to make her case.

"Look," she said sadly while showing him one of the paintings. "I must be depressed. The painting consisted of a flaming red sunset viewed from the heights of a mountain. "There's a black abyss." Carrie reasoned as she pointed to the shadowy depths at the edge of the cliff.

"But look," Dr. B. responded. "There's a little bush."

Sure enough, in the darkness of the slope she had painted a small green shrub, having overlooked it as she instinctively moved towards her freedom. He liked Carrie's work and told her how much he appreciated the chance to see her paintings. The weight from Carrie's shoulders lifted, when she found that someone seemed willing to help her follow her truth, even in the darkness.

Chapter Nineteen

So close

And yet, so far

Tune Reference: *MacArthur Park*

----Jimmy Webb

LATER IN THE autumn, Carrie invited Brent along for a drive to a state park, located only two hours away. He arrived at the house early on Saturday morning.

"What do you call it?" Brent asked when Carrie led him to her car parked in the garage.

"The Blue Mongoose," she replied as she loaded a box of picnic supplies into the trunk. Meanwhile, Brent scanned the perimeter of the car's exterior surface. The car had a cobalt blue body with a silver top.

"I like mongooses," Carrie explained, crawling across the driver's seat to unlock the passenger door for Brent. Brent settled into the bucket seat beside her and Carrie assumed her position behind the steering wheel. Then she started the ignition and backed out of the driveway. Glancing sideways to watch for traffic, Carrie noticed the puzzled expression on Brent's face. She inserted a cassette into the tape player and elaborated further as the music signaled the beginning of their trip, "They're cute, cuddly, and kill pit vipers. Many homesteads in Africa raise mongooses as pets."

Time passed quickly as the Blue Mongoose meandered through the numerous small towns marking the way to the state park. After an hour Carrie and Brent switched positions behind the wheel, allowing Brent to drive the Blue Mongoose into the state park while she gave directions. Once inside the state park, Brent and Carrie chose a three mile trail which interlaced the Brazos River and crossed the park's historical point of interest, the dinosaur tracks lying at the bottom of the Brazos. Intent upon keeping pace with each other's speed, Brent and Carrie hiked the first mile together in silence. When the trail opened to the river bank, affording a panoramic view of the scenery before them, Carrie relaxed immediately and recalled the day's celebrated magic. "Did you know tonight was Halloween?" Carrie asked, admiring the splash of fall colors on the Indian summer day.

"No," Brent answered, jumping onto a log to prevent his feet from getting wet.

"A friend is throwing a party tonight. That's why I remembered. Would you like to stop by her suite afterwards?"

"Sure." Brent always seemed game for almost anything.

"This day seems too lazy for it to be Halloween," Carrie remarked. Maybe that's why there aren't very many people in the park. Usually this place is swamped with visitors. In the summer the park has one of the best swimming holes in the area, but I never knew how beautiful the area became in the autumn season!" she exclaimed while foregoing Brent's course across a log for a jaunt over some nearby rocks.

"Yes, it's very peaceful," Brent agreed. He picked up a few stones and skipped them across the river. "After I get my masters degree, I'm going to get a farm."

"Really? I'd like to live on a ranch in the country," Carrie said with a sigh, recalling the details of her dream.

"I want to have Jersey cows because they produce the best cream. I'd raise wiener pigs and the hens that lay colored eggs."

"Colored eggs! I thought that only the Easter bunny did that trick!" Carrie laughed.

"My dad raised some South American hens that actually laid colored eggs. Besides, I also want some llamas."

"Llamas! Why llamas?" she asked, finding that Brent owned a gold mine of interesting ideas.

"Llamas can be raised as pets and they are good back packing animals for rugged mountain hikes. In addition their coat can be sheared and used like lamb's wool."

Carrie nodded her approval of his pragmatism. Now it was her turn. "I'd like some sheep, goats, horses, an Irish setter, and two Siamese cats. I like Irish setters because they are so playful...Siamese cats have the most personality."

"How many kids?" Brent asked.

"Oh, probably about four," she carelessly offered. "Two boys and two girls. Kids need lots of playmates." Captivated by the splendor of this ideal day, she granted herself the luxury of temporarily ignoring the issue of world population.

"I'd give all my kids the task of milking the cow in the morning," Brent chirped. "There's nothing like waking up at five in the morning to milk the cow. My brother, sister, and I took turns when we were growing up. Many times I'd awake with my head lying against the warm side of the milk cow, while my hands mechanically performed the routine of squeezing milk from her teats. The milk was warm to my touch and sometimes I'd squirt some of the cats who happened to be wandering around the barn...Never seen happier cats, and they looked so ridiculous with the white milk splashed all over their faces. They licked themselves dry." Then he looked down and studied his limbs. "Because this chore strengthens only certain muscles, my arms looked like Popeye's with the forearm being larger than the biceps. My fingers can still remember the motion. It's as automatic as riding a bike." As he spoke Brent demonstrated his skill on an imaginary cow hoisted before him in the midair. Meanwhile, Carrie noted the graceful interplay of the rippling muscles in his fingers and arms.

"I'd teach all my kids how to enjoy the water," she happily announced, recalling the feeling of buoyancy. "I'd introduce them to the water as soon as possible and we'd all swim together like a bunch of ducks."

"I have a difficult time in water," Brent said without realizing that he had implied himself. "Whenever my eyes get wet, my eyelids become crusty and my vision is impaired. I have some special drops that I can use, but I really don't enjoy the water."

"Oh," Carrie said sympathetically. "Have you tried goggles?"

"No, but I'm still leery of getting my eyes wet."

Carrie shrugged and observed the sand bar under their feet. Brent had indicated that he could be a big baby. She couldn't imagine anyone allowing something to interfere with their swim life. She decided not to hold it against him.

"And the T.V. set must go into the basement, so that the kids will watch it only when they are willing to brave the cold room," Brent continued despite Carrie's revelation.

Suddenly Carrie realized that they had unconsciously lapsed into the specifics of raising kids without any formal arrangements and smiled in amusement. Apparently Brent wasn't listening to what he implied. Rather than call attention to this significant detail, Carrie continued playing with their harmless dreams. She had yet to reconcile with the fact that she dated a non-swimmer and a man who didn't care much for dancing. How could she even imagine marrying such a man?

"That's what Daddy did for us. We had to watch Saturday morning cartoons in the basement, otherwise we probably would have watched T.V. all the time," Brent excitedly rambled. His earnestness compelled Carrie to smile in spite of her seriousness.

"I agree. Kids need to learn the value of active play," she continued. "One of the biggest problems today is the fact that we live in a passive society. There's no real interaction with the environment; people wait to let events happened to them instead of exercising some intention in their lives...We'll buy tinker toys and erector sets which stimulate imagination and creativity...and we'll let them have a pet of their own once they become responsible enough to care for it."

"They can have teddy bear hamsters," Brent gleefully interjected.

"Hamsters!" Carrie protested. "All they do is get fat and have babies. We'll have real animals like cats and dogs."

"Teddy bear hamsters are different," Brent insisted. "I had one that would fit inside my shirt pocket while I did my homework. Sometimes he'd stay on my shoulders where I could feel his soft fur brush against my neck."

"Well OK, teddy bear hamsters...but only if they help with homework," Carrie conceded.

"Each kid can have their own room and they can decorate it anyway they wish. Parents, of course, have veto power...I painted my room at home blue. I carved a hole in the wall for a secret hiding place and covered it with a plate for an electrical outlet." Remembering the details of his ingenuity, Brent became silent for several seconds before some insight disturbed his countenance. "I wonder if Daddy ever figured out why that outlet never worked," he thought out loud. He stopped suddenly in this steps with the realization that his secret might not have been as clever as believed. "We'll have a solar house with a greenhouse for plants," he rebounded, sensing that Carrie would agree with this proposal.

"Gotta have a pool and a basketball court," she added.

"How about a pond?" Brent asked.

Carrie informed him, "I like to swim all year."

Soon they became exhausted from fantasizing and contentedly pursued the trail ahead. After rounding several more bends and twists in the trail, Brent and Carrie finally reached the site of the dinosaur tracks.

"Look!" Carrie yelled as she stepped into one of the tracks at the bottom of the river. It had been a dry summer and the water stood only a foot and a half high. "This guy's foot is four times bigger than my own...but then I have small feet for my size," she acknowledged, closely examining the curvatures in the limestone bedrock.

"A vegetarian dinosaur was eating over there," Brent surmised from notes on a wooden trailhead in front of him. Then he pointed to an area on the limestone bank. "A carnivore entered the scene from here. He attacked the dining vegetarian. But he ran into another hungry carnivore that happened to be standing there," he narrated.

"Looks like there was a squabble over dinner reservations," Carrie commented when she observed the resulting mesh mash of tracks on the other river bank. "Evidently no one was hurt."

"The vegetarian apparently ran away during the commotion. Once the prey ran away, the fighting stopped," Brent deduced from the sign's information. Carrie peered at the scenery alongside the Brazos River and imagined its appearance sixty-million years ago: vegetation became more lush and green, and the hard limestone transformed into soft mud. Except for these changes, the total appearance of the land was not much different from the present.

Brent snapped a few photos of the area and they returned to the car. Then he helped Carrie haul the box containing picnic supplies to a covered wooden pavilion located a quarter of a mile away from the parking lot. The pavilion sat in a secluded area of the park far removed from the campground area. Several picnic tables existed on the platform, indicating that the shelter hosted many large parties during the summer.

They settled on a table offering some protection from the wind. Dusk came within the next half hour and enveloped the park in fading darkness. Meanwhile, the wind increased its intensity as Carrie and Brent chatted and sorted through the picnic supplies. Under the wind's direction several threatening rain clouds appeared in the sky, forcing Brent and Carrie to pull on their sweaters in the cooler air.

"Tonight, it's tuna and macaroni prepared on the Svea stove." Carrie announced, proudly displaying the Swiss brass stove. She had purchased it secondhand from a friend of hers who was a serious hiker. "This happens to be the first time I've used the Svea. It's the best available in its price range; although, I hear that the stove can be a little cranky at times."

Thirty minutes and a half a box of matches later, the burner sputtered into a constant blue flame. In another twenty minutes the water in the pot started to boil. Unfurling a red bandanna over the table, Carrie produced a small, red glass dove and placed it at the center of the cloth.

"I call it my scarlet peace dove," she explained while lighting the candle inside the middle of the dove's body. "It's my favorite candle holder," she said wistfully. She sighed when the wind blew out the flame. "It's the thought that counts," she added.

Carrie glanced at Brent. The wind had stolen the flame from the candle and placed the flicker within his eyes and heart. Staring motionlessly at the transfigured man before her, Carrie became conscious of the force of wind rustling through the tall oaks around them and the rumbling of boiling water from the pot on the stove. Her heart skipped a beat. The pulsating noises carried Carrie's heart away with their vibrating journey, stripping her of all other senses. "I think the water is ready for the noodles," she murmured. Slowly, Carrie added the final touches to the meal and dished the plates while Brent remained silent. Transfixed by the sounds encircling them, the couple ate without speaking to each other.

After they finished, Brent and Carrie cleaned their utensils and packed the box containing the cooking supplies. Brent silently helped Carrie spread her sleeping bag over the floor of the pavilion for ground cover. Without a single word, they took off their shoes and sat down together.

In the evening darkness they kissed. The wind howled in their ears, intoxicating them with its fervor. Soon they were drawn inside the sleeping bag by the chilled night air. Prompted by the enclosed warmth of their bodies, Carrie helped Brent remove the clothes separating them. Wildly, they reached for each other as the sensation of skin rubbing against skin melted them together. Brent quivered as he touched Carrie, finally satisfying a deep longing to hold her close to him.

The wind lifted the sleeping bag across the wooden planks like a tumbleweed tossed on a desert floor. Carrie's heart danced with the rhythm of the flying motion, finding no limits to the rapture she felt under Brent's tender touch. She gently caressed Brent's entire body with her own legs, hands, breasts, and face. Claiming his body with her kisses, Carrie released the deep feelings for Brent that she had held inside for so long. Tirelessly, Brent hugged and stroked Carrie until she rested in the nest of his long arms.

An hour later, Brent and Carrie left the park in the Blue Mongoose. Still feeling lightheaded from their encounter, she glowed inside like the soft illumined dials on the car's dash. Carrie looked at Brent. He relaxed in the passenger seat, humming softly to the mellow rock music on the tape player. Remembering the spirit of the evening, Carrie could not recall a more beautiful Halloween night than the present.

Chapter Twenty

If given half the chance
Be grounded

Tune Reference: *El Condor Pasa*
----Paul Simon

THE NEXT MONTH Carrie embarked on a rock climbing trip with a group of students from the state university. She had heard about the club from the man who sold her the Svea stone. When the group decided to go to Enchanted Rock State Park, Carrie signed up. Enchanted Rock, a massive igneous complex located in the middle of the Texas hill country, served as a popular, safe destination for many outdoor enthusiasts.

Frasier, an accountant for the state department, organized the remainder of his life pursuing some form of outdoor recreational activity. His parents were avid hikers and his father had recently climbed Mt. McKinley. They taught their children love for the world of nature at an early age; by the age of six weeks Frasier started spending his weekends in a tent. Twenty-four years later Frasier still enjoyed most of his sleeping hours in a tent.

Arriving at Frasier's house by eight on Friday evening, Carrie met Stan and Stacy. Two more friends of Frasier's intended to meet the group at the park on Saturday morning. Stan, an electrician, currently shared Frasier's latest interest in kayaking and climbing. Stacy attended the state university and participated in most hiking and camping excursions. After they loaded the bed of Frasier's compact Ford truck, the climbers began the four hour drive to Enchanted Rock with Stan and Stacy reclined comfortably on the camping gear in the back.

The truck traveled leisurely along the old highway which had been replaced by the interstate ten years ago. The highway passed through many small Texas towns famous for their police speed traps; a driver could never be in a hurry in this part of the country. The warm night amplified the slowness of the drive and they were ready for action once the truck rambled over the numerous cattle guards leading to the state park. Frasier carefully forded the river which crossed the dirt road marking the entrance to the campground. Then he quickly selected a site, parked the truck, and immediately exchanged his flip flops for a pair of hiking boots.

"Time for a hike on the summit!" Stan announced as he hopped from the bed of the truck. "Wanna come?"

"Where's the mountain?" Carrie asked, noticing that Stacy had declined the invitation. At one in the morning, she preferred going to sleep.

"I dunno...somewhere in that direction." Stan pointed to a grove of mesquite trees. "Hey Frasier, which direction is the rock?"

"Over there," Frasier assured them and corrected Stan's direction by forty-five degrees north.

Squinting in the dark direction of the adjustment, Carrie failed to find a form even resembling a mountain. Ignoring this minor detail, she decided to take her chances on Frasier's venture. "Sure, OK," she replied dubiously. Carrie followed Frasier and Stan through the brush, down a gully, and past some more mesquite trees. When they finally struck rock, the men bounded up the steep slope like a pair of rabbits. Carrie played the role of tortoise, keeping the pace in the slippery comfort of her tennis shoes. Without the moon, she could only see two feet ahead of each step. Carrie reasoned that her best choice in direction was up, provided that she didn't walk over a cliff or drop into a crevice. Occasionally she heard a few footsteps to her right, and made a few turns towards the sound's source. Managing to regain contact with the leaders of the scramble without ever having to utter those dreadful words "wait for me" and spoil the excitement, she reached the summit after a seemingly endless series of upward steps and discovered terrain as wavy as a warped table top.

Stealing a few minutes to recover her wind, Carrie placed her hands on her knees and stooped over the earth. Meanwhile, Frasier and Mark excitedly bombarded her with facts concerning the history and composition of the rock. Carrie only caught some of their information in her exhausted state.

"Look! There's a car traveling on the highway. It must be ten miles away and you can see its headlights from here."

Carrie observed the vague reflection of light sweeping across the rock's surface as the vehicle spun around the curves of the highway. The course grain crystals in the granite rock exhibited a fluorescence, causing the entire mountain to glow underneath the light of the stars. She noticed also that the rock had a particular magnetic quality as if the mountain itself grabbed her ankles and held her feet to its surface. Later, she learned that climbers referred to this endearing quality as the feel of granite. Most rock climbing enthusiasts soon developed a craving for this specific rock. Standing solidly above the competing hills in the region, Carrie sensed no hollowness inside the granite mountain. All their echoes broke the silence and bounced off the smooth granite dome.

The evening wind made its presence felt on the top of the mountain, and Carrie saw some clouds rapidly approaching from the south. In the magic of the moment, she watched the cloud vapor swirl before her like dancing ribbons of mist being led by the wind. Carrie's bare arms felt the ensuing dampness and her nose detected water in the atmosphere. Trapped between the earth and sky by a white film, Carrie waved her arms in the cloud around her to mock the floating sensation. She stamped her feet, as if she never had she felt such a pull to the earth. The mountain bonded Carrie to its breast by the shear force of gravity. If she ever lost her place in the universe, this is where she could find herself. This is where she belonged.

They scurried down the slope and returned to the campsite. Carrie assembled her tent in the dark and dove inside her sleeping bag. As she relaxed in the warmth of her shelter, Carrie tried imagining Enchanted Rock as it might appear in daylight. Failing to conjure an acceptable vision in her excitement, Carrie slept the few hours before sunrise.

In the morning the climbers began an ascent on the northern side of the mountain. The northern face rose almost vertically from the terrain, whereas the other three faces were sharply inclined and promised an arduous walk to the top. After her first glimpse of Enchanted Rock, Carrie saw why it had been so difficult to imagine. The rock resembled a moon fragment, which had broken away and landed on the earth. Her eyes widened in amazement when she reviewed the course navigated during the previous night. From her spot at the campsite, people who climbed the igneous complex appeared no larger than ants. In the wee hours of the morning Carrie had hiked much further and than she had realized.

Ed, Frasier's friend from college, joined them and led the morning climb. For the first segment, they planned to reach a small ledge on the cliff located twenty-five yards from their starting position. While Ed carefully chose his route over the face of the mountain, Frasier explained some climbing techniques.

"By just holding the rope in your hands and bringing it abruptly to the side like this...even a child can support a three hundred pound male," Frasier said as he demonstrated the motion.

"And when you climb, pull your body out from the rock. Be like a spider who spaces himself from a surface with the segmented joints of his limbs. Don't flatten your body against the rock," he advised.

"Every beginner should have at least one test fall to develop trust in the safety rope," Stan aded with a shy smile. It helps you learn how to deal with your limits and survive panic in an emergency. Learning how to fall safely and recover is tougher than learning how to climb, although a fall is easier to perform."

Frasier climbed the slope, replacing Ed at the four inch ledge. He secured the harness around his body to a chock planted in a rock crevice. Then he held the safety rope while Ed began another ascent.

When Carrie's turn came to climb, she fastened her harness to the safety rope and tugged gently to remove the slack. "Belay up!" she yelled to Frasier.

"Ready!" Frasier responded after adjusting his firm grip on the safety rope.

She chose a small indenture in the curvature of the rock and placed her fingers against its edge. One foot found a small protrusion on the surface. Weighing her toes in the groove, Carrie lifted her body with her fingers. Every muscle strained towards the direction of her fingertips as the balance of her entire stance relied on their force. Carrie pulled her body to a another level of balance, and her other hand and foot searched the rock's face for another hold. Halfway to her destination, Carrie's muscles collapsed from fatigue and she fell. Scraping the rude surface of the rock which had once held her, Carrie swung helplessly in the air.

"Are you alright?" Frasier hollered.

"Yah!" Carrie answered him. "Just testing." Having lost her rhythm, her awkward relation to the slope made it more difficult to finger another hold. Finding it impossible to quit, she pushed further up the mountain. Though the fall shattered Carrie's faith in her grip, she felt compelled to trust herself again. To compensate for her lack of confidence, she became more determined as she started the climb over.

Rather than rely on the rock for support, Carrie mastered the skill of using every curvature in the rock to her advantage with a healthy skepticism of all untried reaches. She crawled her way to the ledge where the others sat, dropping her weary body beside the group. Then Carrie eyed the course which she had just climbed with respect.

After the last member of their climbing party reached the ledge, Frasier opened some cans of chicken spread and they made sandwiches for lunch. Drenched by perspiration in the ninety-eight degree heat, they busily passed canteens of water around the group. Ed dumped the contents of his water bottle over his head, shook it rapidly, and showered the group.

Carrie munched on her sandwich in Ed's water spray and thought about her fall. The experience had exhausted her more than frightened her. The idea of hanging on to the world by a string intrigued her. Graphically, this image reminded Carrie of the circumstances delivering her to the clinic only two months ago. *Could always count on that string to be there?* Such a delicate tie to earth seemed too fragile. Carrie scaled the edge of the cliff with the memory of the scene implanted in her mind. Having focused on the climb, she missed the beautiful view, which would have served to distract her efforts. In the exhilaration of the ascent Carrie forgot her scraped knees, bruised shoulder, tired muscles, and sopping forehead. She emerged from the depths with a new perspective, shielding herself from the effects of her grueling efforts. A silent agreement formed between the mountain and Carrie: as long as she maintained faith in her capabilities and trusted the physical sensations of her body, then she could climb it without any trouble. Having learned from failure, this sense of a renewed and stronger individual propelled Carrie gracefully over the threshold leading to the top. At the top Carrie eagerly surveyed the mountain scenery. What beauty surrounded her!

"Hey, you looked like a natural!" Stan yelled.

Carrie had flown over the ascent with the ease of a winged bird. Entranced by the inspiring view, a part of Carrie's spirit remained climbing the mountain forever. She would always cherish the mountain scene. While the physical strains constantly reminded Carrie of her mortality, she touched immortality through her ecstasy. This interplay of immortality and mortality made motion on the mountain possible, and Carrie never would have been able to complete the climb without having first reached the undying spirit inside herself.

As she surveyed the pastel colored hills in the distance, Carrie felt the familiar pull from the granite dome. The rock harbored her in a renewed presence like a lover. Later she left the summit with the others, feeling that she had won a steadfast friend for life.

Chapter Twenty-One

Honesty comforts

In a forsaken world

Tune Reference: *Honesty*

----Billy Joel

SPELLBOUND BY THE wild beauty of Enchanted Rock, Carrie arranged to camp there during the Thanksgiving holidays with Brent. Located only two hours away from her grandparents' house, Carrie planned to camp at the park the night before Thanksgiving and spending a portion of Thanksgiving day with relatives. Then she could return to the park and enjoy rest of the weekend in the quiet hill country. These options gave her more time with Brent without overwhelming him with family introductions.

Brent arrived early Wednesday evening and helped Carrie check the engine timing with a new tachometer which she had recently purchased. Satisfied with its working condition, they loaded the car and began their journey to the state park. In the ebbing darkness of the night Carrie and Brent took turns driving through the sleeping towns along the country highway, while the familiar soft glows from the car's instrument panel provided a constant light inside the car.

They reached Enchanted Rock at eleven o'clock and felt the wheels of the Blue Mongoose rumble over the cattle guard marking the entrance. After selecting a campsite in the midst of a mesquite grove, Carrie parked the car along the dirt road and hopped out. Without bothering to set up camp, she retrieved her hiking books from the trunk and began putting them on. "It's a tradition among the best hikers to climb the mountain as soon as they arrive in the park," Carrie informed Brent, who had followed her around to the trunk of the car. "...In spite of the hour."

Brent eyed Carrie curiously and grinned, "You're crazy, lady."

"Not really. I just prefer learning from healthy risk and practicing the lively art of being able to laugh at myself," she told him, knowing that she had an agreeable cohort. "Not everything in life is contrived. I climbed it at two o'clock in the morning with the hiking group from the state college. The view is wonderful at night, especially when the Milky Way is out. Just follow me. The mountain is somewhere over there." Carrie pointed vaguely to her north and Brent didn't question her direction. Noticing that he seemed willing to follow her almost anywhere tonight, Carrie shook her head and looked at the ground. She reasoned that she could made her way to the summit if she just walked through the park long enough, Carrie led Brent through some brush, down a gully, and past some boulders until they struck solid rock. Then they started to climb.

"It's just right over these boulders," Carrie assured Brent as she hurdled over the next incline, relishing every stretch of her road weary muscles. Brent crawled after her, rapidly shortening the distance between them with his lanky frame. When they reached a point on the slope where they could stand upright, they scurried to the top. Thoroughly exhausted, Brent and Carrie sat on the granite dome and surveyed the serene darkness around them.

"Doesn't this pink granite rock have a magical feel?" she asked him.

"I feel like I'm sitting on the moon," he observed.

"Wait until you see it in the daytime. It looks like a giant moon rock," Carrie told him.

The hike down the slope of the mountain proved much easier than their ascent. Carrie remembered the way and found the established trail. When they returned from their midnight hike, Carrie immediately began the task of setting up her tent in the dark.

"I brought my tube tent," Brent announced. He ignited the carbide in his miner's lamp and flooded the entire grove with its light.

Carrie paused before the fiberglass poles that she had placed around the circumference of her tent. She glanced at the flimsy sheet of orange plastic that Brent unfolded from his kit bag. When his hand pulled out a spool of kite string from the bag, indicating the main support for his tent, Carrie addressed his inexperience with the Texas elements. "I don't think your Vermont tent will hold in this Texas wind," Carrie observed watching the lamp flicker underneath a gust. His camping gear seemed more suited for the sheltered hearth of a pine forest. It would never hold its own in the company of the short, stocky oaks, mesquites, and southern red cedars which withstood wind storms deep in the heart of the Texas hill country.

"I think you're right," he replied, frantically trying to shield his lamp from the breeze. "We can use the tent as a ground cover."

The light from the lamp survived only a few more minutes longer and Brent and Carrie pitched her tent under the light of small flashlight. Then Brent spread their sleeping bags over the floor of the tent as Carrie secured the remaining gear outside the tent.

"Did you know that in the Comanche Indian culture it is the women who own the tents?" Carrie asked, recalling what she knew about some of the earlier wanderers of the region. "If the relationship didn't work out, the woman simply placed the man's things outside the tent, and the Indian brave collected his things and looked for another woman with a tent. A woman chose a man by putting his gear inside her tent and this signified to the community that he was no longer available," Carrie explained, coming terms about her feelings about Brent and setting terms.

She entered the tent and crawled towards her sleeping bag. Already, Brent had casually stripped to his underwear and arranged his bedroll on the floor. Dumbfounded by his nonverbal message, Carrie watched him coyly slip inside his sleeping bag as if nothing was unusual about his skimpy attire. She blinked at him in amazement. "Uh, I thought you wore shorts for sleeping..." she murmured.

"No, I always sleep in my underwear," he assured her.

Carrie crawled inside the tent and gave him a long kiss. She needed no further invitation. Encouraged by his scantly clad body, she allowed his hands to undress her during the warmth of their closeness. She felt him clothe her with his soft velvet skin, making her only vaguely conscious of her nudity. Then he lifted her head above his chest and whispered, "You're beautiful."

Captivated by the gentle blue in his eyes, she quietly told him, "You're very handsome." Her glance fell across the contours of his male body as she spoke.

Suddenly some low cries from outside the tent interrupted them. "Brent, listen! It's coyotes!"

Several mournful howls echoed through the grove, piercing the rustling wind with a lonely bass.

"They must be at least a mile away. I wonder if the ranch owners can hear them...Do the howls bother you?" she asked, curling around in Brent's arms.

"No."

"Me neither, I rather like the sound. It seems comforting in a strange way. Like a baby crying itself to sleep...Do you think they're calling their mates?" Carrie asked as Brent made a trail of warm moist kisses across her. Aroused, she tingled with delight as Brent hiked across her body, causing her to forget the coyotes.

Carrie reached for Brent and rested his head between her breasts as he stroked the inside of her thighs. She held him close, feeling his head rise with every heavy breath until the sensation became unbearable and her body bounced uncontrollably. Feverishly, she drew her hands around his buttocks and tenderly tamed his maleness with her desire. Feeling the energy surge through his body, she released her hold and pulled his body over hers. Together they rode their Throughout the night Brent and Carrie caressed each other. Catching only a few hours of sleep in the early daylight, they awoke in the middle of the morning. Then they ate a quick breakfast, loaded their camping gear in the Blue Mongoose, and began another hike on Enchanted Rock.

They ventured to the same spot where they had climbed the previous night. Brent appeared puzzled. "It didn't seem so deceptive when we climbed it last night."

"Ignorance is bliss. I would have been more intimidated in daylight," she said with a chuckle.

They continued hiking around the northern face of the mountain and discovered a frog pond. Afterwards they walked the angled slope of the eastern side of the mountain and explored a small cave hidden in the rock's core. Leaving the top of the mountain from the west side, they came across a group of giant boulders scattered on the slope.

"You seem so much more confident and relaxed when you are hiking," Brent commented as Carrie skipped over the nearest boulder.

"I feel much more comfortable being outdoors and away from home," Carrie agreed as she leaped across a few nearby rocks to test her restored physical prowess.

Late in the evening, Brent and Carrie left the park for the gathering in San Antonio. About halfway through the trip the Blue Mongoose began to sputter. A sickening rattle clinked from underneath the car's hood. "Sounds like a cylinder," Brent suggested, slowing the car to ten miles per hour. Carrie hurriedly analyzed the situation from her passenger seat. They were miles away from a phone and most stores would be closed at this time of night. Help seemed remote for the present.

"If I slip the clutch and drive real slow, then we should be able to continue driving with minimal damage. Also there's the possibility that the heated cylinders might stick if we cool the car too rapidly by stopping."

"OK. Let's continue at a snail's pace. We'll get there eventually," she decided, accepting Brent's solution.

They reached the outskirts of San Antonio by two in the morning. By now the temperature of the car had cooled to a safe range. "There," she announced as Brent slowed the car. "We are safe here. Ditch the car behind that sign and pitch the tent beyond those trees. Although we're only a mile away from a major university, no cop will bother us if we avoid the highway."

They erected the tent in a live oak thicket about twenty-five yards away from the car. Before settling inside the tent with Brent, Carrie walked back to the Blue Mongoose to check it for the night. Before locking the car, she retrieved a bottle of champagne from the trunk.

"I saved this for a better occasion, but I decided to open it before life became too complicated this holiday season," she explained. Brent smiled at her spirit. Unable to find another container, they took turns sipping the champagne from a plastic cup.

"I propose a toast to life's ironies: Celebrate the fun we enjoyed before the car broke," Carrie offered, raising her cup before sipping some champagne. She handed the remainder over to Brent, who returned her salute. "I'm not looking forward to facing the family," Carrie confessed as she began tearing away at her clothes. "It's not the car that bothers me. I suspect that my mother had someone tinker adversely with my vehicle."

Feeling the winter air slap her like a cold shower, Carrie savored its chill. She desperately needed to feel its stark reality. When the feeling became too much to bear Carrie blocked the sensation, allowing the cocky spirit of the champagne to deaden the cold for her.

"My relatives are just waiting for me to break," Carrie grimly stated. "My mother told them that I had suffered a break down before going into the hospital. She never told them the real reason, because she has something to hide. Now I have to play dumb so that they don't get upset with me. I know the drill."

Calmly, Brent began removing his clothes. Carrie blinked at him in amazement, feeling awed by his quiet gesture. Without a further word she put away the bottle of champagne. She decided to maintain calm alertness. Then she laid down at the opposite end of the tent, resting her head on her upright arm. Surveying Brent's body from toe to head, she discovered a special closeness which would have been spoiled by physical contact. His entire body radiated a magical warmth towards her, soothing her bared soul.

"Honesty is a lonely word," Carrie recalled, citing the words of a song. "And I need the truth." Carrie rearranged her position such that she laid her head directly beside Brent's.

"What is honesty?" he asked.

"I never really knew until tonight," Carrie replied like she often did with her younger sisters. "I've been remembering the words of a song. I think honesty is like being naked without feeling ashamed or vulnerable."

"Like being naked," Brent softly echoed before closing his eyes with a contented, knowing smile. He had begun to fall asleep when the discussion grew philosophical. Almost mechanically, he reached out his long arm and pulled Carrie close to his curled body. Once safely nestled in the cavity of his velvet chest, she recalled the loneliness of honesty. Carrie realized that she did not feel alone when she shared her thoughts with Brent.

At six o'clock the same morning, the Blue Mongoose rolled into her grandparents' driveway in time for breakfast. Fortunately, Carrie's grandfather knew a reliable mechanic who could fix the car in town. Brent and Carrie deposited the Blue Mongoose at the mechanic's garage by eight that morning and returned to her grandparents' house.

Meanwhile, an uncle had informed Carrie's mother of the situation while Brent and Carrie were at the garage. When Carrie arrived at the house, her mother cornered her in an empty hallway.

"Now I don't want you getting upset about this," she scolded Carrie. Without altering the amount of venom in her voice she quickly changed the subject, "My boyfriend and I are going to the market this afternoon. Do you and Brent want to come along?"

Heading frantically for the nearest exit, Carrie said with a shrug, "Sure, we'll come."

As soon as they arrived at the market Brent and Carrie left her mother and her mother's boyfriend, and arranged to meet them later. Not interested in shopping, Brent and Carrie bought a few Mexican cookies and sat by a secluded public fountain.

"She responded exactly as you anticipated," Brent observed after Carrie mentioned the morning encounter with her mother.

"Yes," she gulped. Long overdue tears began streaming down her face. Carrie brushed them away and stared blankly at the water fountain. Tossing a few cookie crumbs to some begging pigeons, she watched her fine-feathered friends scurry like slap-stick comedians for the morsels. More tears fell from her eyes, as she remembered *The Comedians.* "Oh no," she said with a sigh. "Well, I suppose it's alright to cry here."

"It's OK," Brent assured her, pulling Carrie gently towards him with his arm wrapped around her torso. She buried her face in Brent's shoulder and sobbed.

"I'm sorry," she said.

"What for?" he asked.

"For the weekend, for the car, for crying...," she quietly blubbered.

Brent whipped a crumpled green bandanna from his pocket, and happily dotted the tears away from her face. Then he held his handkerchief and coaxed Carrie to blow her nose. His fussing made Carrie smile. "The car wasn't your fault...And it is OK to cry. Girls are supposed to cry. My sister does it all the time. Boys often wish they could cry, but people won't let them...I can tell you about all the cars that I've had with blown cylinders...And nobody touched them; they fell apart on their own..." Brent's version of the world brought an even bigger smile from Carrie. "Now look, you're smiling again, lady," he beamed, encouraged by the obvious success of his efforts.

Carrie rested her head on his shoulder and listened to the crystal rhythm of the water as it trickled over the glistening blue tiles. She did not feel like talking anymore as a few more tears escaped her eyes. They threw more crumbs for the pigeons and watched them fall over each other on the slippery tiles like a circus. No finer entertainer could have matched the pigeon's routine; they served as the true clowns of the city. In the company of fools, Carrie felt encouraged. "Well, I'll probably sell the car to help pay for repairs and use the remainder to go away to college. I'd like to finish my physics degree," Carrie ventured, attempting to make the most of the situation.

"Now it looks like something good will come of this after all," Brent brightened, exuberantly wrapping his long arms around her in a mighty hug. Being a physics major himself, he secretly nourished a desire for Carrie to join him in his academic pursuits.

Carrie slightly smiled and squirmed underneath his arms. Brent's embrace told her that he was someone with whom she could honestly cherish, an immeasurable worth from her standpoint. Serving as another benefit of the weekend mishap, the realization shattered any illusions concerning her family and she needed to change.

Chapter Twenty-Two

There's a lot to be said

For freedom and the pursuit of happiness;

People have died for these supreme values

Tune Reference: *Me And Bobby McGee*

----Kris Kristofferson and F. Foster

ONE WEEK AFTER the Thanksgiving holidays, Carrie sold the Blue Mongoose and enrolled in a state college almost two hundred miles away for the spring semester. Frasier and several other members of the outdoors club were alumni of the East Texas college and they recommended the school for the large number of environmentalists among its student population. Boasting a large forestry department which ranked third in the nation, the college's research played a vital role in the development of the local timber industry. Carrie eagerly looked forward studying forestry along with her physics curriculum.

The Christmas holidays arrived shortly before Carrie finalized her college plans for the upcoming new year. Brent and she spent Christmas day at her grandparents' and then left for a week long camping excursion. They hiked three days in the desert near the famous Judge Roy Bean saloon and camped at a state park chosen for its historical Indian caves and hieroglyphics.

At night temperatures plummeted down to below freezing from a daytime temperature in the eighties. The Svea stove didn't operate below thirty degree temperatures and they gathered mesquite wood to cook over an evening fire. The mesquite provided a hot smokeless flame and added excellent flavor to their canned meals. Coming quickly with the winter hours, darkness prevailed at the evening meal and compelled Brent and Carrie to retire early. After dinner they took turns tending the fire while the other person showered at the public restrooms.

"You know I could hear "Battle Hymn of the Republic" a quarter mile away from the showers. You're getting better!" Brent greeted as he approached the camp site during one evening. During his absence Carrie had found her harmonica inside her backpack and had tried harmonizing with the rustic environment.

"Thanks. Actually I think it has something to do with the desert acoustics. The tones sound more mellow," she said before playing "Dixie" and "Yankee Doodle" for their cactus audience. These melodies comprised the only three songs she knew on the mouth harp. Although Carrie felt more comfortable fingering her guitar, she had left the instrument at home because of its bulk.

On the fourth day they drove through a desolate portion of west Texas and visited some caverns, acclaimed as the most beautiful in the world by the World Spelunker's Association. The caverns did not disappoint Brent and Carrie, and the formations proved much more spectacular than any they'd seen at other underground caverns. Leaving Sonora in the early afternoon, they traveled further down the highway until reaching another state park, an area haunted by local ornithologists for the diversity of bird species inhabiting the park's numerous southern red cedars. They hiked around the park's lake for several hours and spent the remainder of the day lounging in a hammock which Carrie suspended from the limbs of two oak trees.

Two weeks later, Carrie left for college away in east Texas. Brent had offered to drive her there and she accepted, explaining that the trip would be less stressful than a bus ride or a ride with her mother or Ellen. When Brent and Carrie had driven a hundred miles outside of the city, they encountered hazardous road conditions. Snowfall from the preceding night buried many of the small Texas towns in a white blanket. Lacking the resources necessary for maintaining the highways under these conditions, driving became treacherous until the snow and ice melted. With the most of the car's weight distributed on his rear wheels, Maxwell excelled on the slippery roads.

Much to Brent's delight, the tiny VW bug passed mighty trucks and many cars with four wheel drive that tried crossing the iced hills. Driving in the snow reminded Brent of his home in Vermont, and he seemed to appreciate the exercise in nostalgia as well as the opportunity to boyishly challenge his car in these conditions. When they arrived in town, they found the campus almost void of staff and students. Because of the snow storm, the college had closed and cancelled the first two days of classes. Many students remained snow bound and would not return to campus until road conditions became better.

News of a second impending snow storm limited Brent's stay to only one hour. They said their good-byes at the snow covered parking lot near her new dorm. Carrie wiped a few tears away and explained, "I'm going to miss you very much."

"Ah..., I'm going to miss you too. I'm going to have brownie withdrawals now that you're away," Brent replied as he leaned out the window, sweeping Carrie in his arms. "What do you mean? You've got me hog-tied and corralled," he smiled, squeezing her tightly.

"Good!" she suddenly burst. More tears trickled down her face.

"I'll write you when I get back to the university," he assured her before he started the car's engine.

"OK," Carrie told herself as she pulled away from his arms and straightened in front of the car's door. "Promise me you'll take care of yourself and drive safely."

"I will," Brent grinned while revving Maxwell's engine. Then he backed out of the snow covered lot and drove onto the main street.

Carrie waved at him and walked towards the dorm. She sensed that Brent and Maxwell would be safe on the icy roads, possibly safer than she in the nearly vacant women's dorm. With Brent and some luck, she started to overcome the odds against her.

Chapter Twenty-Three

Destiny doesn't always explain
Or make sense for the moment

Tune Reference: *I Can't Hold Back*

----Survivor

COMPARED TO THE university, student life at the state college seemed sedated. There were few practical jokes performed on campus, and individuals easily conformed to convention. People maintained their distance from each other and the pursuit of learning was viewed more as a business than an active endeavor; classes ended within prescribed hours with minimal rapport between teachers and students. Consequently, Carrie made the adjustment to the large campus with relative ease because the large campus offered much more autonomy. She always had the personal freedom, at least, to make her individualized learning experience as worthwhile as she wished.

Enrolling in a few Forestry courses to satisfy her yearning for the outdoors, she learned how to identify trees by their twigs and cones. The lab instructor led the class on hikes throughout the area to collect samples. For tests he'd point to some unobtrusive stick barely making its way to life from a crack in the sidewalk and ask the class its genus, species, and common name. Enjoying the hikes, her short term memory struggled to retain the information. The shock of recent experiences had not worn off. She scored much better on physics tests where she could think her way through problems with minimal amount of cramming.

Soon after classes resumed for the semester, Carrie applied for a job as a Physics lab instructor. The young man who supervised the physics labs appeared very bright and congenial. "Ever taught a laboratory course?" he questioned her, rocking back on his chair. Several lures from his fishing hat brushed across his face when he moved.

"No, but I have ten years of experience in teaching swimming lessons," Carrie answered.

"It's all the same," he said straightening in his chair. "They either swim or drown. OK, you're hired."

She enjoyed her job very much, though initially it demanded valuable time from her studies. Eager to complete her physics degree, Carrie jumped ahead in her curriculum without bothering to complete the prerequisites and this doubled the time she spent preparing for her classes. Brent came for a weekend visit after classes began. He stayed with the boyfriend of Carrie's roommate, who rented a house with three other men. Another small world, the boyfriend was the younger brother of a mutual acquaintance at the university. Brent had stayed with this family during his trip to Houston. In addition, Carrie constantly ran into many familiar faces from the area high schools in Dallas and Fort Worth. There were even a few individuals from her grade school. Her date for the senior prom also appeared on campus one day and they resumed their friendship. Dividing her life into two distinct segments, Carrie discovered she enjoyed studying with the physicists, but preferred socializing with the Forestry department, the most outdoor group on campus.

Two weeks after Brent's weekend visit, Carrie hopped on a greyhound bus bound for Dallas.

"How's it going, lady?" Brent greeted Carrie as she met him at the terminal.

Without saying another word Carrie threw her arms around the circumference of his skinny body. She felt so happy to see a familiar face among the rogues loitering at the bus terminal. From all appearances, Brent fitted in well with the environment. Wearing his leather jacket and black sailor's cap, Brent's thick unruly hair and bearded face seemed a threat to the rougher looking characters and they carefully avoided him. Hanging onto his arm as they made their way out of the crowded terminal, Carrie felt like she nothing to fear.

"I gotta get back to work soon. There's a program that I need to start running in another hour," Brent announced once they were outside the dingy building, near where she had once met the therapist and psychiatrist. "What are your plans for this weekend?"

Besides his regular campus jobs, Brent worked as a night time computer operator. A glorified babysitting job paid by oil companies tracking their well production, Brent's tasks consisted of running a few programs and calling the supervisor whenever the computer crashed. He shared the position with two other students from the university, and the position often allowed time for sleep and study during working hours.

"Well, I'm here to see you. I'd just as soon avoid seeing my folks if you don't mind," she said, looking around at the familiar surroundings. If her mother decided to look for her, this would be her last guess. "I feel safe right here in the middle of things. Mind if I do my schoolwork while you watch the computer. I have lots to do."

Brent happily grinned. He certainly would not mind her company during the lonely forty-eight hours he spent operating the computer. A city built by commuters, downtown Dallas transformed into a ghost town on weekends and she wandered through vacant streets and offices during trips for hamburgers. The atmosphere of the empty city relaxed Carrie because she didn't have to contend with the hustle and bustle of crowded city conditions. At night she curled beside Brent on the floor to the office and slept between program runs. The machine clanged and whirled computer printouts throughout the night, stopping only when it was time to change the operation. In spite of the noise and discomfort, Carrie smiled, expressing appreciation for the time with Brent and accepted the circumstances as a luxury.

Awaking early on Sunday morning, the day of her departure, Carrie discovered Brent missing from his place beside her. She immediately glanced towards the computer. She sighed with relief when she spotted him laboring over the printer. No longer in her tiny dorm room, she took full advantage of the building's architecture. She rose from the floor and opened the window shades. A brilliant city sunrise greeted her, flooding the room with its brightness and warmth. Relaxing her shoulders, a curious sense of homeowners' contentment filled her as she viewed the scenes below with the eyes of an eagle. Almost considering herself the richest person on earth, she fathomed that those who inhabited the building during regular office hours didn't know what they missed. It wasn't just about her.

When it came time to leave for the Dallas bus terminal, Carrie gathered her things from around the room and packed them in a small overnight bag. Tying the strings around her overnight bag, Carrie felt a sudden sinking feeling seize her chest. Confused by the sudden emotion, she collapsed in the chair behind her as she stammered quietly, "Brent, I feel like my heart is breaking..."

She shook her head over the feeling. It didn't make sense. She could take care of herself. She would see Brent again some other time. However, telling herself these things didn't subdue the swirling sensation which poured from her heart and into her head. The feeling became too much to bear and Carrie began weeping, burying her head in her hands. She felt caught.

Brent came and put his arm around her. "It's OK," he comforted Carrie, tightly holding her hand in his. Carrie began shaking involuntarily as the tears streamed down her face. He moved forward, holding her close to his body where her face fell against his chest.

"Something is wrong," she gasped in bewilderment. "I can't go today, I'm too upset."

"It's OK, it's OK...," he soothed Carrie. "How about if I drive you back to school?" He gently removed Carrie's hands from her face and looked directly at her. Carrie nodded, feeling helpless in the situation.

"Do you mind?" she questioned.

"No," he smiled. "That's what I'm here for," he answered while hugging Carrie tightly. "We'll go after I finish this program."

The time for departure arrived quickly, and Carrie's tears returned once they started driving. Without speaking, she merely laid her head in Brent's lap. Nobody on the road could see her. Brent hummed softly as he watched the traffic, placing his hands around her waist in reassurance. Emotionally exhausted, Carrie fell asleep for the duration of the trip. By the time they reached the campus Carrie felt ready to resume her college activities and leave Brent.

Two weeks later, Brent returned to campus to visit Carrie.

"Guess what? I have a surprise for you!" Carrie told him when he arrived on Friday evening. "I rented a cabin in the National Forest. If this weather ever clears, we can do some hiking."

Unfortunately, the rain persisted throughout the weekend and thwarted their hiking plans. Nonetheless, Brent and Carrie found plenty to do in their cozy environment. She cut his hair; they took a shower; they caught up on their sleep; and finished their homework assignments.

Chapter Twenty-Four

Be wary of those moments

When you must assume the initiative

For your life as well as future

Tune Reference: *While You See A Chance*

----Steve Winwood

PLACING THE LATEST letter from Brent on top of her books, Carrie sank into her desk chair and remembered the time spent with him over the weekend. She read Brent's letter again. He seemed depressed. He wrote about the long hours at his jobs and his worries about saving enough money. In contrast, her sleep cycle began to resemble that of a vigilante. Tensions remained in the air.

That night Carrie attended a movie on campus with several other women who shared the dorm hall. The movie, a French film narrated by a French psychologist commenting on the case studies of three individuals.

"Every creature is a product of its environment," he began. It has basic drives for food, sleep, and procreation. Environmental stimuli elicit responses from living organisms consistent with these basic drives. If the stimulus is negative, then the animal will respond negatively to its environment," the psychologist explained.

The following scene showed how rat behavior could be modified through a punishment and reward system. A scientist placed a piece of cheese at the other end of a maze. Every time the rat chose an undesirable path, the animal received an electric shock compelling the creature to choose the correct one. In the second scene a rat received an electric shock every time he tried to eat a piece of cheese, so that the rat associated eating with pain. As a result, the rat suppressed its drive for food and died from starvation, dramatically verifying the psychologist's prediction. Next the psychologist correlated the studies to human behavior, analyzing typical everyday situations in light of the proposed theory. After one scene showed an argument between two lovers, the next clip exactly repeated the encounter with rat heads and tails substituted for the corresponding human forms. All human reactions became the equivalent of programmed rat behavior: anger reacted to anger, insults responded to insults, and negative stimuli evoked negative actions. Other scenes showed how human behavior could be manipulated through a reward and punishment system, using segments from the lives of the three individuals as examples.

According to the psychologist, these case studies supposedly represented the norm in the human species. One man, numbed by his environment, mechanically assumed the role of businessman, husband, and father with the precision of a programmed robot and the range of feeling of a vegetable. The second individual, a woman, endlessly sought fulfillment through a perpetuating series of love affairs. The third person responded to his environment with the act of suicide. Finally, the movie ended with the psychologist's summary, the same as the name of an intramural football team of upperclassmen at the university: "C'est la vie" or "Such is life."

Feeling as if the carpet had been pulled from underneath her, Carrie left the theater feeling bewildered by the scientist's assertions.

"That movie depressed me!" roared the business major in her small town accent, breaking the silence as they walked together towards the dorm.

"I'm not sure I understood it," the language major admitted, being an honor student.

"All the characters apparently lacked the vision needed to rise above their circumstances," Carrie offered.

"What do you mean?" the business major questioned, pursuing the issues even further.

"It has to do with the ability of an individual to break the mode of predictable behavior rather than just respond passively to life," the language major who also could speak French.

"Hmmm," the business major said with a grinning nod. She seemed satisfied with the interpretation.

Encouraged by the language major's words, Carrie attacked the movie's theme like a debater, "If we don't agree with the psychologist's initial presumptions concerning life, then we can toss out the case studies. They are probably biased anyways...Look, human beings have more opportunities than rats because life is not always as defined as a maze. Common sense says that the psychologist's analogy is not valid."

"Hey, you're right. His arguments sounded so convincing that the plot's basic premise slipped right by me," the language major confessed. Taking a deep breath, she expressed relief that the source of the depression had been exposed.

"I feel manipulated," the business major said with a sigh.

"The movie manipulated the audience," Carrie observed. "The psychologist's approach left no room for discussion."

"I suppose that we're so accustomed to accepting these things in our classes that we never bothered to question the movie's plot," the language major commented.

"Seems that the majority of society as a whole agrees with those views," the business major added.

Carrie added in amusement, "Tomorrow I could walk into my Modern Physics class, watch the instructor close his book shut, and hear him say, 'Sorry folks, we came up with something else. Everything learned so far has been proven incorrect.'"

Both the Language and Business majors smiled, conveying their preference for stability. Together they spent over an hour rapping about studies, then Carrie returned to her room and continued her homework. Carrie's roommate was out. She spent a major portion of the semester at her boyfriend's house which often afforded Carrie the privacy of a single room. Carrie rather enjoyed the solitude; if she ever desired company, she could just open her door.

Still concerned with the movie, Carrie gave up concentrating on her physics assignment. She laid her pencil down and rose from her chair. Staring out the window from her room on the parking lot.

Time to get out of the rat trap, she thought, feeling her lower jaw stiffen. Carrie checked her window view and peered between the closed slats of the shades. The parking lot had cleared and no one seemed to be watching her section of the dorm. She glanced at Brent's letter which remained opened at the far corner of her desk. Feeling a resolute strength stir from her gut emotion, Carrie determined how she would respond to Brent's letter.

The next night Carrie carried all the loose change that she owned and ran across the parking lot to a store pay phone. Holding her breath until she heard his familiar voice answer the phone, Carrie greeted, "Hello, Brent!"

"Hello lady! How are ya doing?" he asked her with the usual vibrancy.

"Ah, Brent, I think we should get married," Carrie softly whispered.

Chapter Twenty-Five

Sometimes you have to love

With your head

Tune Reference: *Sonnet CXVI*

----William Shakespeare

"ARE YOU SURE? Do you know what you're saying, lady?" he asked breathlessly. His voice inflections told Carrie that he smiled at the other end of the wire.

"Yes."

He quizzed her, "Do you know what you are giving up?"

"Yes."

"Do you know that I can't offer you much right now besides myself ?"

"That will do."

"Do you know you might have to quit school for awhile and follow me around?"

"Sounds good. I'm prepared for that."

"Reserve the cabin and I'll arrive as soon as possible on Friday afternoon. We've got lots to talk about and lots of planning to do. Don't worry about anything, lady. Brent is magic; I've got lots of tricks up my sleeve."

"That's why I'm calling, Brent. I wanted to get this issue in the open so that we can work together."

Late Friday afternoon Carrie heard a knock at her door and rose from her desk to meet the caller. It was Brent. For a brief, uncertain moment in time Carrie's and Brent's world stopped, and almost an hour passed without their knowledge. When she regained awareness of their present surroundings, she whispered to Brent, "I think we should probably leave soon." In spite of their feelings for each other, both knew that they would not consummate the relationship before marriage. To Brent and Carrie intercourse appeared as a curiosity, looming ahead in their future like land on a sea horizon. Wrapped tightly in the emotions of their romantic interludes, they remained content with the amount of sex in their love life for the same intangible reason that lovers such as Romeo and Juliet never consummate their feelings until they reached the right place in time.

When they reached the cabin, Brent knelt on the floor of the kitchen and took Carrie's hand. "Carrie, will you marry me?" he burst with a smile.

"Brent!" Carrie shrieked. The traditional proposal had caught her off guard.

"I was going to wait until I could make you a better offer."

"This is the twentieth century," Carrie pleaded, looking directly into his eyes as he stood. Then she told him, "Yes."

Having completed the traditional formality, Brent sat down at the dining table and Carrie immediately bounced into his lap.

"What next?"

"We could elope."

"No, my parents would be disappointed."

"Mine would sigh with relief. How about just before graduation?" Carrie asked with her brow furrowed. The graduation could serve as a distraction and their enemies would not be able to get past the surrounding crowds. You're folks will be there and we could invite our friends from college. Your father will appreciate the savings in money, and he wouldn't need to make more than a single trip."

"Sounds great. We have two and one half months to get ready."

"Alright. I'll handle invitations, check into the legalities, and plan the reception."

Brent handled the rest, choosing to attend graduate school in San Antonio where he planned to pursue engineering. Proceeding with their tentative plans, Carrie took a weekend bus headed for Dallas and together they called Brent's father from the university dorm.

"I thought your father was joking, until your letter arrived," she later apologized. "All he said was that you were getting married before graduation. You know how your father is. Now I'll have to call everyone and tell them that it's true. Daddy gets to foot the phone bill for this prank," she remarked with laugh.

However, Carrie dealings with her mother weren't as humorous. Two weeks later, she told her family during spring break when everyone had gathered around the dining table for lunch. Not surprised by the news, her mother dissuaded Brent. "She doesn't cook and she does very little housework."

"Brent doesn't push me out. Besides, the car will be maintained and the yard will look good."

"Boy, I'll say...," Ellen interjected. She rolled her eyes as she spoke, emphasizing the ridiculousness of the entire discussion.

The mother glared at Ellen and continued, "Carrie would not make a very good wife, and she doesn't have much to offer. I hope you know what you are getting yourself into, Brent."

Carrie decided to defend herself with humor. "Ah, Mom," she insisted dryly, "I am very good at making chocolate chip cookies. We'll live on those until Brent and I figure out the rest." Sandy giggled and Brent smiled.

Carrie's mother looked very unhappy. "Well, I know you both love each other," she conceded.

As a result of the tension at her mother's house, Carrie changed her plans for spring break and left earlier than originally intended. The next morning Carrie and Brent drove to the Gulf coast where they camped on the beach with hundreds of other college students. On the way back to school they stayed overnight at a campground two hours away from college. One of Carrie's acquaintances from a college came over to introduce herself, while Brent collected wood for a campfire.

"Still teaching yoga and aerobics?" Carrie asked as the older woman sat down on a log and sipped her beer.

"Come and join us, when you have a free moment, she offered. "I heard that you were getting married."

Refusing a beer, Carrie sat down on the log beside her and gazed at the other campers in the area. Some prepared for a party, while a few stole away for contemplative hikes. "My period kicked out under the stress, but I'm not pregnant," Carrie admitted. "It's somewhat hereditary. My great aunt, an army nurse, lost hers in World War II." Pausing for a moment, Carrie stared at the dirt floor beneath her bare feet.

"Mind body connection," the yoga instructor commented.

"My mother wants me to see a shrink."

Her friend laughed, tossing off the notion as she savored her bitter. With chagrin, she commented, "It's poison."

"I know."

Becoming more philosophical under the circumstances, she advised, "Run."

"I tried that."

"You're mother doesn't want you to grow up."

"She needs a garbage can that she doesn't have to take out. I refused to be their sacrificial lamb, or the chess king in their game of armageddon."

Suspending her brew in the air for a brief second, the woman gulped. "Those who borrow against the future of their children cannot contain the spiritual wine. They lack the faith needed to deal with events as they appear."

"Like Noah, after the flood?" Carrie questioned. "It's spiritual incest."

The woman rose as Brent entered the campground with a pile of wood. Making a quick exit, she heartily shook his hand and told him, Congratulations."

Later in the week, Carrie checked with a specialist. He asked her whether she ever had intercourse when he became upset over his findings. "Ever had anything violent quite some time ago?" he asked with anger and irritation before his voice trailed off.

She merely shook her head as he gently questioned her. He wanted to meet Brent on a followup visit. The next week, Carrie ushered Brent inside the office. She gazed at the poster on the wall of a half nude boy carrying a daisy in his hand. Compared to the sterile, power-play offices of the prior physicians in her life, this younger professional expressed dedication to innocent displays of affection between genders. This contrasted greatly with the room of the women across the hall; they hung full length posters of denuded men on their walls. Though Carrie never broached the assault on sensitivity directly to the women, she gained the confidence of the other women in the dorm. Being more familiar with the anger and bitterness of the rooms inhabitants, everyone except a few brave men avoided the area. The male callers that knocked on Carries door served to neutralize the aggression of the self-righteous three feet away. In the judgement of those sentencing their neighbors, Brent seemed only part of a river defusing the blatant, defiant hostility.

As the physician answered a few questions about their future plans and answered questions concerning birth control, Carrie fathomed the juxtaposition of images that life had presented her. It appeared that he just wanted to see Brent and Carrie together. Although most of the conversation seemed rather inconsequential, Carrie welcomed the opportunity to involve Brent who appreciated his inclusion in a world often cloaked by feminine mystique.

"I'm now a man of the world," he happily observed after they left the medical building. "Even the guys at school treat me with a different sort of awe and respect."

Carrie laughed. "It's within my best interests to keep you informed as our potential family may require your support and understanding.

Carrie's appointment with Dr. B. also proved inconsequential.

"What brings you here? I told you that I didn't want to see you in my office again. He said with a nervous smile.

"I'm getting married to Brent and my mother wants me to check it out with you. She thinks I'm sick. I must be ruining her alibi."

Dr. B. grimaced and looked down at his desk for a few moments. "There's something about the capacity to love which measures sanity," he murmured. Facing Carrie, he met her eyes and stated emphatically, "The problem is your mother's."

Having heard the unspeakable, Carrie silently nodding and accepted his assessment. He abruptly resumed his professional demeanor, he straightened the papers on his desk and stated in a businesslike voice, "If she questions you further, have her call me."

Another matter crossed his mind and peered at Carrie with his eyes opened wide. "Uh, I understand your conservatism and religious upbringing as well as your own personal sense of morality...uh...have you and Brent been...uh...intimate?" he asked, pausing for a moment to search for the right descriptive words.

Intimate? Carrie swallowed hard, bracing for a lecture on fornication. Then she spoke truthfully in the words of her young generation, "Yes, but we haven't gone all the way. We're happy just being together."

"Good! Good!" he joyously exclaimed. "Intimacy is very important in a relationship. One should feel comfortable with their partner before choosing to spend the rest of their life with them."

Though, she could not imagine marrying a man without having been intimate with him, her shoulders relaxed with the support from a man older than her father. She nodded at Dr. B. She had sensed the importance of intimacy and had never fully realized its value until now.

Chapter Twenty-Six

An essence of a rose

Moves people forward on a slippery slope

While supporting and stabilizing

The mind-body circuits of

Evolutionary growth

Tune Reference: The Rose

----Bette Midler

SLOWLY, BRENT AND Carrie resumed interaction with the world of dates and schedules that they had known before the wedding. In the warm, congenial atmosphere of the physics and engineering programs, Carrie and Brent created their first home together. The had adjoining desks in the same student office building on the third floor. Like other students in the department, both married and single, they helped establish the interdisciplinary associations into one family. During the summer following the school year, Carrie instructed a Physics lab and earned class credit for her independent research in electronics. She increased her physical stamina to the point where she could play on the women's intercollegiate soccer team in the fall semester. She also enrolled in some advanced geology courses and made close friendships with a few of the other students.

"Why doesn't San Antonio celebrate *Cinco de Mayo?* The celebration is gaining popularity in Seattle," one graduate student commented during lunch.

"That's because it is more than just chips and salsa," Carrie quipped as she gathered the books for her next class.

"Ah yes, it is the thorn on the rose that pierces the armor of the human heart," another graduate student rejoined. He smiled as he leaned back in his chair for further discussion.

Carrie looked down at her collection of notebooks. Choosing her load carefully, she elaborated, "The English department just tenured a Graham Greene scholar." Turning to face the confused student directly, she asked, "Ever read *The Comedians?* Isabella-Spain has been collecting human hearts for a very long time now. The people who live here are too heartbroken to dance with the celebration."

Then she turned on her heels and left the rest to the reclining graduate student to explain. In the evening, she joined several classmates at a geology review hosted at one of the rentals off campus. The host lived there with his housemate, another geology major. They had shared many adventures in the past together and earnestly crammed to pass the latest round of tests.

"OK, what is a geosyncline?" the host asked in his most serious voice, while his mustached grin betrayed his playfulness. As soon as he gave the correct answer the host continued with his study questions for tomorrow's Stratigraphy test.

"OK, what time in the morning do you get up to go duck hunting?" the host questioned in the same serious voice. In the later hours of the night, both the questions and answers rapidly became nonsensical.

"Duck hunting! I gotta get my hat to answer that one!" his housemate yelled. Both housemates ran from the table and returned quacking to the living room wearing their fur-covered caps.

"Five o'clock in the morning," the housemate insisted after the two men settled at the table like a prepared comedy routine.

"Correct. OK, Carrie, draw a thrust fault on the chalkboard," the host instructed, finally eliciting a smile from Carrie before she walked over to the board hanging on the dining room wall. Appreciating the softer side of these muscled men, Carrie noticed that they seemed rather anxious in expressing their sensitivity. Looking at the chalkboard over the dining table, she took a deep breath and relaxed her shoulders to offset the tensions in the air.

"Does it matter what color chalk I use?" Carrie teased, admiring the selection at the board. The remark gave her more time to think about her answer, especially since geologists focused more on earth-bound details than physicists. Shaking her head at soft pastels, she realized that the pursuit of science could be an artistic endeavor.

"Use the different colors for the ages of the rocks," the host firmly explained, before waddling over to the board. "And I'll draw a syncline. I just know the prof is going to ask these questions on the test. Quack. Quack."

"Did you know Karen is looking for another apartment?" the housemate asked before he drew his geologic structure on the board.

"Oh, really?" the host said without conviction. Then he angrily threw his piece of chalk at the base of the chalkboard and straddled his seat at the table. "I can't blame her, especially since they haven't caught the guy who raped her roommate."

"He held a knife to her throat. She couldn't escape," he said with a shudder. "Shoot, I wouldn't move either if someone stuck a knife at my throat."

"Instead of studying, the other men in class are on the lookout for that critter. They will kill him if catch him before the police. How can anyone do such a thing? I hope they catch up with him."

"Some people are strange. Just like our peeper."

"Did Jack and I tell you about our peeper?" the host excitedly asked Carrie excitedly.

"No, you didn't," Carrie answered after overhearing the men's discussion. Unlike the other university, they openly verbalized their feelings about such events, instead of joining in the mayhem or burying the issue in denial. A knock on the door interrupted her thoughts.

"Come in!" the host hollered, before he stormed into his bedroom. He left the housemate and Carrie to greet the late caller. Another classmate, a tall, burly man, entered the living room and waited for the host to arrive. "I'm returning your geology notes," he announced, handing the papers over The host, who had just retrieved his pistol from his room, took the papers. He laid the pistol on the table in front of burly gentleman.

"What's that for!" the man cried, shocked by the gun openly displayed in front of him.

"I'm gonna use it to scare away our peeper," the host replied. "I don't want him peeping around here. He might came back armed."

"Find the one who raped the roommate," the man growled. "There's too many of those kinds of people in this city. No one is safe anymore."

Then he sadly shook his head and searched Carrie's face for compassion. She backed away and the host turned his head away. "I don't know what this world is coming to," he said softly.

"Well, if you shoot someone don't forget to drag the body inside the house and place the gun in the dead man's hand. You don't want to be the one thrown in jail. The laws are pretty funny these days," the burly man remarked.

"I'm not sure I could shoot someone except in self-defense," the host with the pistol decided as he glanced towards his housemate, and consulted him as if he served as his conscience.

"There was a fellow in my high school who shot a burglar in his house," the burly man recalled. Leaning back on his heels, he felt the weight of the memory. His shoulders slumped forward as he stared at the floor. "And the boy seemed never quite the same afterwards."

Tossing a shoulder at the men gathered around the pistol, Carrie ignored these wealthy, young men. "I could do it." Given a little money for a license and gun, she could give up her studies for another calling. Familiar with this terrain from the violence she had previously witnessed at home and school, she confidently eyed the cold-steely weapon. Before her mother had caught her to teach her how to read, she had hid in a juniper bush with her metal pistol, a weapon that she never treated as a toy. Assignments in first grade had civilized her somewhat.

The host picked up the gun and fingered it for a moment. He studied her face and smiled. Rather than hand it over to her, he simply nodded and kept it in his hands. Satisfied with Carrie's answer, the tall man left. The housemate peered through the shades and watched his car roll out of the driveway. Then we waited for a few seconds at the window before announcing, "Our neighbor has a good-looking woman with him."

"He's too ugly to have a girl like that," the host decided with indignation, after he joined his housemate at the window.

The sound of pounding fists erupted from the other side of the duplex wall. The two men echoed the pounds from their side.

"Good luck on tomorrow's test!" Carrie shouted above the din as she hurried out the front door and hopped inside Maxwell. Declining to stay and meet the neighbors, she drove to her garage apartment only a few blocks away.

Arriving home at one o'clock, Carrie discovered that Brent had already quit studying for the night. He had left the light on in the kitchen for her before going to bed. Carrie stepped across the stones on the walkway leading to the apartment and brushed past the bamboo lining the path. In comparison to the fraternity, he slept in a naive and nonviolent world. She entered the house, securing the locks behind her until she had made her way to the hide-a-bed in the studio room.

Chapter Twenty-Seven

No armor, no walls,

No castles needed

Except to shut out world chaos

And serve as symbols of success

For those having endured difficult lives

In bleak terrain

Tune Reference: *The Wall*

----Kansas

AFTER THESE MEN graduated, Carrie continued her studies, conscious of being both stalked and tracked by people connected to her parents. When uneasy dreams and feelings began disrupting her sleep at night, she consulted a college counselor and told him about him about a baby blue negligee that her father had sent over the holidays. "I threw it in the garbage. It seems inappropriate for our relationship. When I called and asked him about it, he said that his wife had helped him pick it out. I only haven seen his wife twice in my life, one being the wedding. I asked him not to send anymore presents."

"Did your father ever molest you?" he quizzed her.

"No, but I felt violated in many ways."

"Well, what do you think about these dreams?"

"I don't know. That's why I'm here to see you," Carrie told him. Burned out over her parent's dramas that had once kept her up nights, she waited for some tidy answer. As far as she had been concerned, she had lost her family when the skeleton first began to come out of the closet, years ago.

"You're crazy if you don't believe them!" he growled.

Stunned by the emotion behind his words, Carrie questioned, "Are you sure?"

He leaned forward and stated bluntly, "It's obvious that some traumatic event occurred in your childhood that you still remember. It is probably much worse than what you are able to recall. These are powerful feelings. Facing and understanding them is the only way to prevent them from controlling your life."

Leaving the counselor quickly, Carrie briskly walked past the canopy of live oaks on campus. Her shoulders tensed as if she sensed that she was walking into a trap, like a rat in a psychology drama called *C'est la vie*. Waving her hand across her face as if to through off a mosquito, she discarded the counselor's sermon before it became a life sentence. Her thoughts centered on *The Comedians*. Instinctively, she found an approach that would entertain them while she completed her course work.

Like a detached, analytical debater, she spent the next few days preparing a response for the counselor. Using her ability to throw herself in a trance, she described the memory of an attack in a language that would cause the fascist philosophers to ponder. She invented a story about a bird with a taboo, such that even its mother wouldn't touch it. Then she made the analogy between the story of the bird and computer programming. In this manner, she escaped those who thought that they could program her like a Manchurian Candidate, except she would not be the assailant. Instead, she would be sacrificed in the manner the Spaniards turned virgins into drug addicts before publicly carving out their hearts. Like the poem that she had presented to the hospital staff, the analysis that she later presented to the counselor served to release her from those pursuing her since childhood.

Some of the people that harangued her during aerobics class volunteered to help her with Project Kill Bird. Wrapped in their religious beliefs, they passed judgement on Carrie without taking the time to get to know her or befriend her. The busy daughter of a preacher enjoyed solving everyone's problems, except her own. When Carrie unwittingly became one of her targets, she dodged the religious persecution by balancing the fanaticism against the counselor's deceptive net. His spider's net came from the fascists, who had secured places for certain Nazis officers a few months before World War II ended. They eliminated targets through strings of lies and deceit.

After recalling the experience under self-induced hypnosis, Carrie solicited the preacher's daughter and boyfriend as her witnesses. These witnesses disarmed the counselor's rabid approach and diffused his insecurities about women majoring in physics. About a brief lecture about how he and his wife gardened with the man officially planting the seed, he dismissed Carrie.

After the final visit with the counselor, Carrie went home and gardened for the rest of the afternoon. She had planted her own seeds before reaching childbearing years. She weighed the ways that people seeded in life. Sometime during the negotiation with the counselor, the religious woman from aerobics had become pregnant by her dark-skinned lover. She had been pressured the into an unplanned pregnancy, and she had lost the baby. In the heat of the dramas, the anger and rage directed at Carrie lessened considerable as the couple became lost in a self-inflicted vortex. Meanwhile, Carrie focused on keeping Brent safely tucked in his secure world. She maintained cover as the devastated, helpless young woman majoring in physics, playing college soccer, working part-time, and running a home as wife.

She had moved on, while her father still wanted to put her in a blue nightgown and send her to bed. Regardless of having been used by military powers attempting to control her parents during the time of the assassinations, Carrie dropped the entire affair and avoided the net that had been used to setup her parents. Faithful to the big picture, she visited a friend, who had decided to get married on the east coast. Feeding the counselor unrelated information had made it safe for Carrie to travel. Her friend, Donna, had eluded capture from the fascist spider's web encircling Dallas. After the trip, Carrie resumed her studies in the south.

Louise, the roommate of the preacher's daughter sought Carrie's companionship as the spinning webs began isolating people on campus. While spending an afternoon assisting her in the library dark room, Carrie told Louise about Donna's wedding on the east coast and summed up the liaison with the campus counselor. "After doing a meditation with the light of a candle, I realized that the skeleton in the closet reminded me of the K of O fraternity, which is a kin of an east coast diversion called skull and bones. The complete skeleton appeared in my dreams as a warning to get out of California. It occurred a year after RFK's murder."

"Skull and bones. Some people even call it an organization," Louise quipped, shaking her head. She changed the subject with the hint of emerging excitement in her voice. "You don't live near that closet anymore, though this campus is filled with official groups with lethal, sexual rites. Here, take a look at this." Being a major in nautical astronomy, Louise pointed at some photos taken from her studies off the Greek Islands. She had worked briefly with Yanni, the head of research there. Yanni also had attended Donna's wedding at the invitation of a close friend.

"These photos remind me of what we found in the MidEarth," Carrie commented. "The geologists tell me that Freeport Sulphur has been accused of polluting Barton Springs in Austin. The company played a role in JFK's visit to Malaysia."

"The British patriots are still looking for Ponce de Leon's Fountain of Youth."

"But, we have it right here in Barton Springs."

"I know. They also connect with the shipping industry operating out of Turkey."

"They are a bunch of illusionists, who run Russia's KGB courtesy of the post-Atlantean crystal embedded in Malaysia."

"Now you see it; now you don't," Louise reflected with the hint of a tease in her voice.

Hearing someone enter the office, the women quieted and ended their discussion of the darkness that literally enveloped them. Momentarily trapped in the room, Louise nervously glanced around her for a change in subject matter. She quickly produced some pictures of her recent hike in Colorado. In the photo, she held a camp robber in the palm of her hand. Taking a moment to admire the masked bird, Carrie studied the flight in the next photo. The camp robber flew higher and higher toward the snow-capped mountains in the distance. Looking at the clear blue sky, Carrie could sense the spirit of the tiny bird. Meanwhile, Louise gathered her belongings and they stepped outside like two chums gossiping over vacation photos. They side-stepped the researcher in the nearby room and exited the building.

Stepping outside to the shadowy gray confines of the parking lot underneath the library, Louise and Carrie paused and examined their immediate surroundings. They discreetly parted with a silent wave of the hand. Louise opened the door of her sedan in the underground parking garage, while Carrie headed for the bike rack outside the Science building. She bicycled home without any further revelation until reaching the familiar driveway that led to her apartment. Safe at home, she weighed the latest intrusion on her psychic space in the dark room in light of her recent conversation with Louise.

As she reflected on these more significant events, Puddy, the cat that lived in the garden gracefully wandered toward her. The cat purred and demand to be caressed, reminding Carrie that the need for affection held the same importance as stopping to smell the roses. All these pieces of her mirror instinctively formed the archetypal divine presence she sought. Like the Blue fairy of her dreams, which protected her soul, the cat's presence warmed and inspired her. The thorns of life served to pierce the armor that she reluctantly carried, and betrayed her human heart. With the wispy castle on the distant horizon, she choose to live outside its wall as she pursued greater security in the gathering world chaos.